Hands-On English Teaching

A Complete Guide with Classroom Management Techniques

演練式英語教學：班級經營策略全指引

- A Powerful and Dynamic Instructional System
- Increase Student Speaking and Writing
- Help Students to Become Fluent in English

Alex Rath

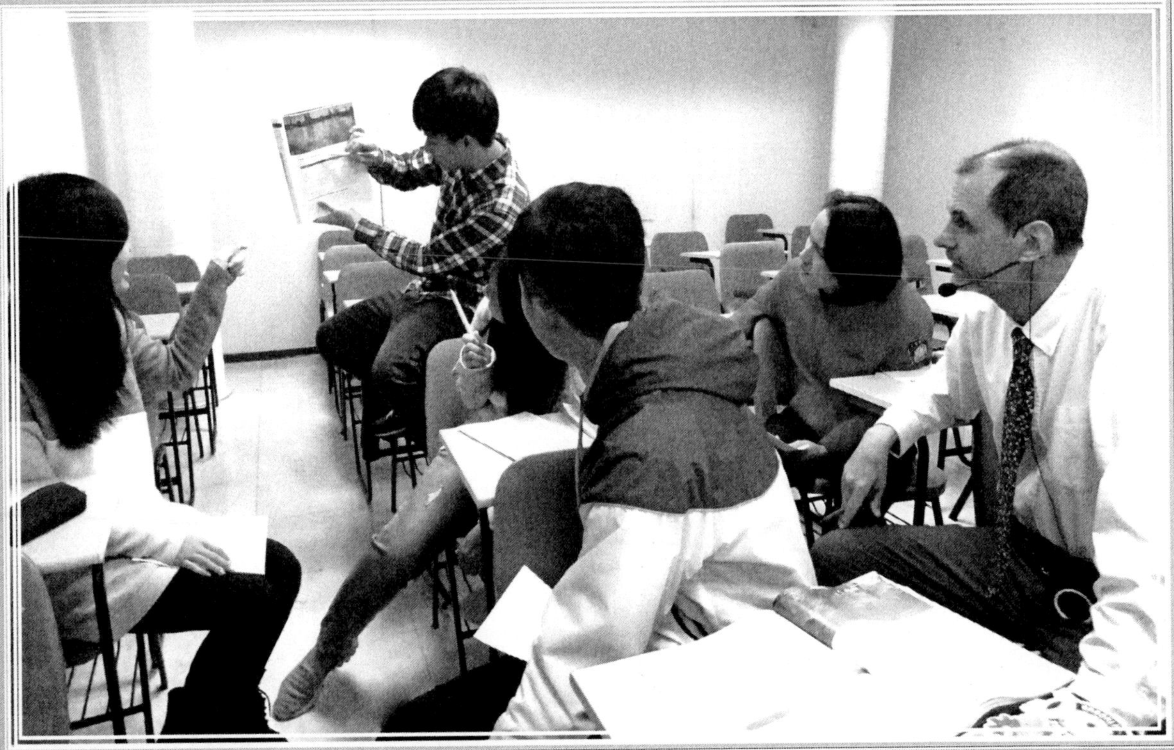

Hands-On English Teaching: A Complete Guide with Classroom Management Techniques

Illustrations by Emily.
Photographs by Cyndy and Mark.
Published by Rath Media Co., Ltd.

Printed in Taiwan, Republic of China
Distributed by Elephant White Cultural Enterprise Co., Ltd.
Elephant White Cultural Enterprise Ltd. Press
8F-2, No. 1, Keji Rd., Dali Dist., Taichung City, Taiwan 41264 ROC

ISBN: 978-986-98298-0-9
Suggested Price: **NT$250**

Table of Contents

Introduction

Part I: Setting Instructional Stage

Lesson 001: Introducing Hands-On English Teaching 20
Lesson 002: Starting on Time 22
Lesson 003: Assigning Seats 25
Lesson 004: Introducing Yourself 29
Lesson 005: Discussing Class Time 31
Lesson 006: Discussing Attendance 33
Lesson 007: Discussing Breaks 35
Lesson 008: Stating Class Rules 38

Part II: Preparing Classroom Structures

Lesson 009: Greeting Students 42
Lesson 010: Monitoring Late Arrivals 44
Lesson 011: Banning Distractions 47
Lesson 012: Projecting Lesson Plans 50
Lesson 013: Quieting Down a Class 52
Lesson 014: Checking Textbooks 55
Lesson 015: Collecting Student Data 58
Lesson 016: Making Biopages 60
Lesson 017: Making Biobooks 64
Lesson 018: Updating Biobooks 66
Lesson 019: Requiring Header Paper 69
Lesson 020: Explaining Homework Procedures 71
Lesson 021: Collecting Secret Codes 73
Lesson 022: Describing Online Document Submission 75
Lesson 023: Explaining Paper Security 77
Lesson 024: Requiring Document Filenames 79

Lesson 025: Demonstrating the Upload Process 81
Lesson 026: Collecting Paper Copies in Class 83
Lesson 027: Collecting Classroom Data 85
Lesson 028: Writing Teacher Notes 88
Lesson 029: Managing Student Data Spreadsheets 90

Part III: Running Participatory Activities

Lesson 030: Requiring Classroom Contribution 94
Lesson 031: Selecting Student Presenters 98
Lesson 032: Guiding Student Readers 101
Lesson 033: Guiding Student Writers 105
Lesson 034: Guiding Student Computer Operators 109
Lesson 035: Writing Lesson Plans 112
Lesson 036: Selecting Textbook Activities 115
Lesson 037: Incorporating Speaking and Writing 117
Lesson 038: Introducing Mispronunciation 120
Lesson 039: Explaining Mispronunciation 123
Lesson 040: Describing Types of Oral Language 126
Lesson 041: Requiring Complete Sentences 129
Lesson 042: Correcting Sentence Structure Errors 132
Lesson 043: Explaining Evaluation 135
Lesson 044: Displaying Grades and Line Graphs 139
Lesson 045: Trying New Instructional Activities 142

Appendix

3.1 Assigned Seats 148
8.1 Class Rules 149
10.1 Late Student Sign-in Sheet 150
12.1 Couse Schedule LANG107 Spring 2019 151
16.1 Biopage 01 Handout 152
16.2 Biopage 02 Handout 154
19.1 Header Paper Sample 156
19.2 Header Format Instructions 157

20.1 Composition-01 158
21.1 Secret Codes 160
22.1 Online Submission 161
26.1 Audio-01 Assignment 163
27.1 Late Arrivals 166
31.1 Contribution Checklist 167
35.1 Lesson Plan Sample 168
37.1 Class Coverage Tool 174
43.1 Grading Key Example 175
44.1 Grade Spreadsheet 176
44.2 Line Graph with Markers 177

Figures and Tables

Figure 1: The three major parts of the Hands-On English Teaching process.........14
Figure 2: The placement and interaction of teachers and students during a Hands-On English Teaching class..........17
Table 1: The interaction between teacher and students during Part III of the Hands-On English Teaching process..........15

Introduction

演練式英語教學法構思背景

在開始規劃一門英語教學課程時，要牢記的是，學生過去的英文訓練上，比較著重閱讀與聽力的訓練，但是學生需要也期待更多的口說跟寫作練習。在英文課中要符合這個期待是個巨大的挑戰。老師們經常詢問的問題是，要如何在英語課堂上增進口說與寫作的成分，尤其是在大型班級的課堂上。我認為「演練式教學法」可能可以提供一個方法、一套系統，讓英語老師們可以透過引導學生進行課堂參與，來達到增加口說和寫作訓練的目的。

在過去廿年的英語教學課程中，我已經教過二十人至六十人一班的學生口說和寫作，並獲得學生良好的反應。我採用的教學法為「演練式教學法」。此教學法強調師生皆要參予活動。這個教學法我自己簡化暱稱為「粉筆、走路和說話」三步驟教學法。也就是說，老師給予學生一個簡短的演講，然後會在課室中來回走動，檢查學生的作業，並與學生個別談話以及給予協助。跟這個教學法相對的教學法稱為「講台上的智者」,「講台上的智者」是指僅有老師一人在台上教課。雖然這個教學法能學到較多跟主題有關的知識，但學生很少有練習的機會。在「演練式教學法」中，便是要克服這些缺點，因此老師需要減少課堂數與PPT過多的頁數，並設法將學生練習口說和寫作之安排，視為中心要務。

「粉筆、走路和說話」教學法強調課程訊息的傳達、師生間的互動和學生的個別化指導。「粉筆」指的是老師在課堂上所傳達的資訊；「走路」是指老師會走下台，和在座位上的每位學生作互動；「說話」是指老師會給予學生個別指導。然而，在改學生的練習時，可能會讓台上太過空閒。

「演練式教學法」結合老師與學生在台前的練習。有些人可能會認為教師在這樣的課程中可能與過去有很大的不同，改變太大，但這個教學法事實上並不難。在教學過程中，學生會被分到讀者、寫者和操作電腦的任務。他們需要到台上完成這三樣工作，而老師會引導在台上的學生。老師有時候會跟台上的學生一起練習題目，有時候會到台下跟其他學生作互動，在「演練式教學法」中，老師的角色會在訓練在台上的學生完成英文活動以及幫助座位上的學生之間流暢轉換。

雖然這個教學系統中含有大量的演練式活動，包含了許多英語口說課跟寫作的成分，但此課程之規畫依然要從其課程目標開始，並透過實作演練活動來確認學生是否達成課程目標。老師需要在第一堂課向學生說明課程目標跟教學方法。課程目標跟教學方法都講解清楚後，日後上課就不用花太多時間回顧課程結構跟教學流程，這樣就有更多的時間可以進行實作演練活動，讓學生發展其口說以及寫作的技巧與能力。這堂課的教學系統最主要目標是為了讓學生多練習口說跟寫作，次要目標包含各方面能力的提升，如文法、單字、聽力、閱讀、聽從指令以及修飾用字。和傳統課程相比， 演練式教學需要老師跟學生花較多時間參予學習過程。

在老師對學生作個別指導時，老師需要知道學生的能力跟學習目標之間的差距。由於學生的程度不一，大部分學生的課堂表現都未達標準，這時老師需要解釋目標讓學生理解，並且找出學生能力與目標之間的差距之內容與程度。要了解這個差距，老師需要透過面對面一對一的方式，去了解學生的學習狀況以及個別的興趣跟學習動機。實作演練活動對於評估學生的狀況很有用，這個方法比能力測驗更能了解學生能力與目標的差距。了解學生程度跟課程目標後，老師即使在大班課程中，依然可以設計專屬課程和給予學生個別的學習途徑，以協助彌補個別學生能力與目標之間的差距。

課堂管理是教學方法能夠有效實施的基礎。因為增加學生口說跟寫作的練習量是課程的重要目標，課堂管理需要跟教學方法作整合，確保學生在參與課堂的態度由消極轉成積極。課堂管理不僅僅是管理學生而已，課堂管理在大班教學課堂中，創造出鼓勵學生的機制，給予學生能夠獨立練習口說跟寫作活動的支持架構。課堂管理也幫助老師做個別指導。建立一個可以達成目標的教學系統需要設計、發展跟管理許多環節。

融合本書中所提到的「演練式教學法」的教學方法、「粉筆、走路和說話」的教學技巧以及課堂管理等方法，教師在課堂中可以更有效地幫助學生的口說和寫作能力。教師在這樣的課堂上還是可以使用課本。但課本主要目的在於提供系列性的內容，而老師可以將這些內容融入演練式教學法的課程規劃之中。本書中所提到的教學系統之建立，能夠增加學生口說跟寫作技巧的練習機會並達到整體學習參與度的提升。或許要學習這樣一套獨特的教學方法可能會花老師一些時間，但老師們在檢驗結果時，可能會覺得這樣的心力花費是非常有價值的。

Background for Hands-On English Teaching

As a starting point, it is important to keep in mind that past English learning for most students focuses on listening and reading, but students need and want to learn more speaking and writing. It is indeed a daunting task to fulfill this student request. The main question teachers ask is how it can be done, or how they can increase speaking and writing activities in large classes. The answer is to include Hands-On English Teaching activities, an instructional system based on teachers coaching students during practice activities.

In the past twenty years, I have taught speaking and writing in courses with enrollment ranging from 20 to 60 students, and have obtained positive feedback from students. I use an instructional method called Hands-On English Teaching. The name emphasizes active teacher-student-involvement. This instructional system can also be called Chalk, Walk and Talk. In other words, the teacher gives the students a short lecture, and then walks up and down the aisles of the classroom, checking student work and helping students one at a time. The opposite of this method is sometimes called the Sage on the Stage. The sage is the person at the front who delivers a lecture. Although the sage on the stage may know a lot about the content, the students rarely get practice time. Given the shortcomings of the lecture method, teachers have to reduce the number of lectures and the endless PPT slides, and place student speaking and writing front and center. The method Chalk, Walk, and Talk addresses the problem.

Chalk, Walk and Talk is an instructional system which emphasizes information, interaction, and individualization. Chalk is a metaphor which means the teacher presents information. Walk means the teacher walks up and down the aisles of the classroom interacting with students. Talk means the teacher gives individual instruction to the students. However, checking student papers leaves a vacuum at the front of the classroom.

Hands-On English Teaching combines the teacher working the room with student presenters at the front. Some people might ask if the teacher has too much to do in such classes, but it is easy if teachers relinquish the role of Sage on the Stage. Students are assigned jobs such as readers, writers, and computer operators. They are assigned a job, and they go to the front to complete it. Naturally, the teacher has to supervise the students at the front. Sometimes the teacher is at the front working with the students, and other times the teacher is walking and talking. In Hands-On English Teaching, alternating between helping students in the seats and coaching the students completing the English activities at the front is the central role of the teacher.

Although this instructional system is characterized by a large number of hands-on activities, English speaking and writing classes have to start with curriculum goals, and the hands-on activities can help examine if students achieve these curriculum goals. The curriculum goals and instructional methods need to be explained to students in the beginning of the class. After the goals and methods become established, less time has to be spent reviewing curriculum structure and instructional process, and more time can be spent on hands-on activities where the students work to develop English speaking and writing skill. The primary goal of this instructional system is for students to practice English speaking and writing. Secondary goals include improvement in areas such as grammar, vocabulary, listening, reading, following instructions, and word processing. Compared to traditional lecture classes, hands-on instruction requires teachers and students to be more involved in the learning process.

To achieve educational goals, teachers need to individualize. The teacher needs to learn about the gap between student ability and the learning goal. Student ability varies widely, and most have yet to reach or surpass the specified skill in the class. The teacher has to generally explain the goals for the students to understand, and then discover where each student stands in relation to the goal, which means to determine the size and shape of the gap. This assessment of the student gap has to be done face-to-face in order for the teacher to understand the individual learning factors and their mix with other issues such as personal interest and student motivation. Hands-on instructional methods are useful while evaluating the student gap, as they illuminate the gap as much or more than other types of evaluation such as language proficiency testing. By understanding the gap between student skills and curriculum goals, teachers can better individualize instruction in a whole-class setting, and effectively develop individual approaches for all the members of a class.

Classroom management is the foundation on which instructional methods rest. Since the major goal for my courses is increased student language production, which means more speaking and writing by students, classroom management and instruction have to be coordinated to ensure that the students move from a passive to an active level of participation. Classroom management is more than just administration. Classroom management encourages students to participate by creating a framework for their speaking and writing within the overall class structure. Classroom management also facilitates individualization. Building a system that achieves many goals requires that the numerous parts be designed, developed, and managed.

After combining the hands-on teaching methods, the Chalk-Walk-and-Talk technique, and the classroom management process described in this book, teachers will be able to help students with their speaking and writing much more effectively in class. Although most classes have a textbook, it is simply an organized series of content lessons which can be used in a hands-on teaching English class. Therefore, the distinguishing feature of Hands-On English Teaching is the increased student speaking and writing. This unique instructional system is the most important part of Hands-On English Teaching. It will take more time in class, but the results will be worth it.

Instructional Framework

The Hands-On English Teaching System involves not only the instructional techniques but also the process of managing the class. The instructional management can be described as three steps:

- Setting the stage for student readiness
- Designing the activities for participation
- Coaching for students to increase performance

The framework for the Hands-On English Teaching methods, or the model, as presented in Figure 1, summarizes the three parts. Part I, Basic Structure, helps the teachers to introduce the basic rules and structure of the class to the students. The purpose is to set up the stage for the later instructional practice. Part II, Classroom Management, provides a discussion and guidance for classroom management details ranging from monitoring attendances to managing student data sheet. Although seemingly tedious and often ignored, these management procedures are crucial to ensure an effective classroom structure which the instructional method is built upon. Part III, Instructional Techniques, explains the essence and procedure of the hands-on English teaching instructional method.

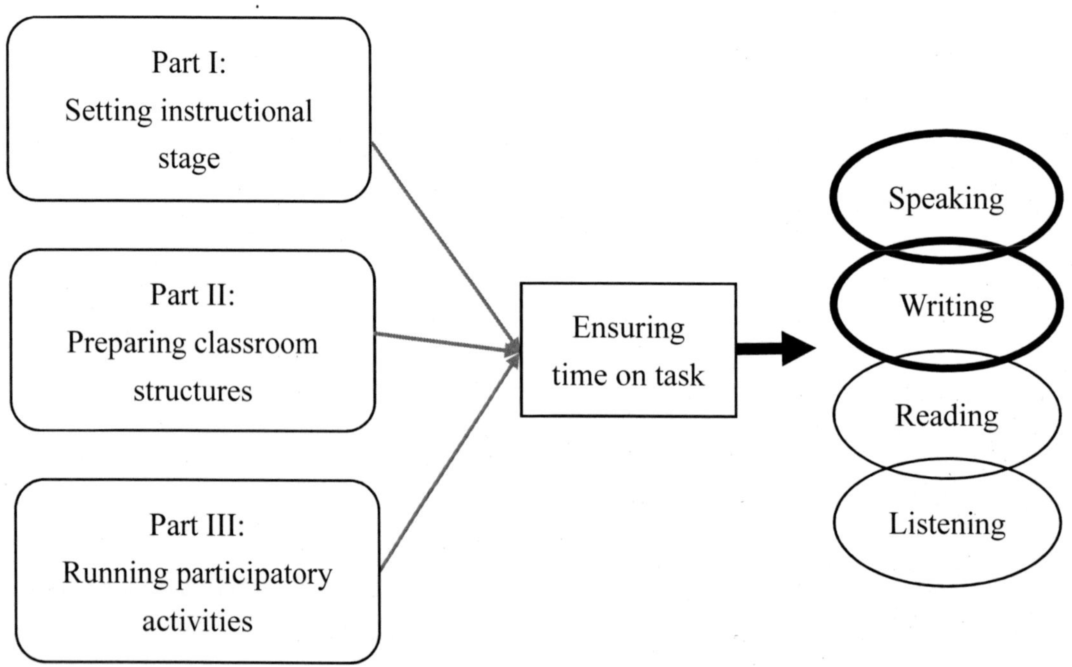

Figure 1: The three major parts of the Hands-On English Teaching process.

Part III, which describes the stages in Hands-On English Teaching process, has several important steps for the teacher to complete while working with student readers and writers. The teacher has to give an assignment that everybody in the class can complete, and then starts the student writer on the production of a demonstration. The student readers are called in to read the student writing. The teacher checks papers and coaches students while the demo is being prepared, and then the teacher coaches the student writers at the front for all to hear and watch. To further explain the participatory process, a description of what the teachers does and what the students do during a writing activity are presented in Table 1.

Teacher Process	Student Process
Review content and assignment, such as writing definitions of vocabulary words	
Assign definition writing job to the whole class	Students start writing
Select two student writers	Selected student writers go to the classroom computer at the front
Start checking the work of students in the seats	All students write definitions
Check progress of students writers	Student writers write the same definitions as the whole class
Continue checking work of students in the seats	
When student writers are done, select two student readers	Selected student readers go to the platform at the front and get microphone
Start review of definitions produced by student writers	Student readers read aloud definitions the writers wrote which are projected from the computer
Coach speaking of student readers	Student readers repeat if they said it wrong, and then sit down
Offer suggestions to student writers	Student writers rewrite definitions if necessary, and then sit down
Sometimes the writer-reader process goes through several rounds of reading and revisions	
Sometimes readers and writers are used separately, instead of going up to the front together	
The use of readers and writers is repeated as needed during class time	

Table 1: The interaction between teachers and students during Part III of the Hands-On English Teaching process.

These are the steps that teachers must take in order to increase student learning through the use of Hands-On English Teaching methods. Teachers guide the students through the process, and the students make the connections and improve their skills. The students have to do the work themselves, so teachers must give them work time and error correction in class. After that the students practice, and teachers coach the students during subsequent practice activities which build on the work they completed. Displaying examples is a good start, but the effort on the part of the students to speak and write using the techniques they are practicing in the key to their progress. The teacher has to see their work as it develops, and right after they finished it, in order for them to better understand the error corrections and practice with the new technique. That is how the Hands-On English Teaching process works.

Classroom Setup

Hands-On English Teaching is designed for the standard 60-seat classroom with a computer, projector, and screen. The standard 60-seat classroom usually contains a whiteboard or a chalkboard, which might be utilized on occasion, but is not an important part of this instructional system. There is nothing about the arrangement of the classroom furniture and instructional equipment in a 60-seat classroom that physically prevents a teacher asking students to go to the front to use the computer and speak on the platform. Likewise, teachers regularly walk around 60-seat classrooms, moving up and down the rows of seats during, for example, exams. Hands-On English Teaching, when reduced to basic teacher movements, is just more time walking around the classroom, checking papers and helping students. The main addition to this age-old teacher behavior is placing students in the front as computer operators, readers, and writers. The management of the classroom process, with students at the front and students in the seats all working on the same projects, requires the teacher to combines coaching presenters with checking papers and guiding individuals in their seats. Figure 2 illustrates this process.

Figure 2: The placement and interaction of teachers and students during a Hands-On English Teaching class.

The Hands-On English Teaching instructional process starts with the teacher introducing content, and it proceeds through student readers and writers to homework and evaluation. When repeated regularly in class, and used to direct homework, this instructional system increases time on task. The increased amount of individualized assistance to students, increased participation of students, and increased time on task all work together to increase student learning.

The conceptualization of instruction may be complicated at first glance. The system involves various basic techniques which many teachers have already been using. The Hands-on English Teaching method extends these techniques and encourages teachers to employ a variety of tools in different situations.

Part I

Setting Instructional Stage

Lesson 001

Introducing Hands-On English Teaching

Hands-On English Teaching is an instructional system for general English classes, which can also be described as four-skill courses or applied English classes. Since students will need some English on the job, the focus is speaking and writing, as students need to develop effective communication skills. Students from all majors take English courses. Teachers select topics and textbook content based on the skill level of students in their sections and their professional expertise. As a result, the content of many general English courses is highly variable. Given the lack of a standardized English curriculum, focusing on an instructional system means that it can be applied to many types of English courses. Not every instructional system works. The Hands-On English Teaching system described in this book requires teachers to coach students during numerous practice activities.

The instructional system in this class, which can be called Hands-On English Teaching, or can be described as "chalk, walk, and talk," can work with any applied English textbook, whether a four-skill textbook or a book which focuses one or two areas, such as a reading and writing textbook. An instructional system is a teaching method, and therefore it can be used with many curriculum areas. In fact, this book is close to a methods class in a college of education which covers all manner of teaching techniques. While no book can replace a four-year degree in education or a graduate degree in English language and literature, this book aims to review all the techniques taught in teacher training classes in an English teaching degree program.

A: Good morning, and welcome to English class.

A: This is a new course.

A: When I say new, I mean new for me, and new for SHU.

A: Since this is the beginning of a new course, there are many unanswered questions about what is best and how to get it done.

A: The focus of this course is speaking and writing.

A: We will use World Class 1B, which is a high-intermediate textbook.

A: We will steadily work our way through the book.

A: The textbook will be the basis for the speaking and writing activities which you will do during class time.

A: This class has a unique instructional system, and it may take you some time to get used to it.

A: The goal of this instructional system is to increase the amount of speaking and writing that students do in class.

A: All the students in the class will have to come up here, to the front of the class, where you will speak and write for the class.

A: Don't worry. I will help you.

A: Since this is probably your last required general English course, the goal is to help you consolidate your speaking and writing ability,

A: The goal of concentrating on speaking and writing is so you can communicate effectively after you graduate and join the workforce.

A: Now, let's look at the syllabus, which you should have picked up when entering the classroom.

A: Does anybody need a copy of the syllabus?

B: I do.

A: It's there by the door. Please help yourself.

A: I put the handouts by the door so students can pick them up when they come in.

A: You have responsibilities. Please take care of the things you have to do.

A: I'll teach the class, and you have to do the work.

A: Right? Right!

Lesson 002

Starting on Time

Teachers should start classes on time, give students breaks on time, and end on time. In order to effectively manage classrooms full of students, teachers need to follow the posted times. Students appreciate teachers who conduct classes with a firm hand. That is not to say that a teacher has to be heavy-handed. The issue is structure, and it has to be clear and stable. Students want to know the ways that the class works, and they want the system to be handled fairly and consistently. This whole process begins with the bell announcing the start of the class session.

When a teacher strolls into the classroom ten minutes late, it is hard to get students to take class time seriously. When classes start with the late arrival of the teacher, especially an unprepared teacher with only a vague sense of classroom management, all teacher authority is lost. The teacher is the role model, and has to set an example. However, modeling on-time behavior is not the main reason teacher should start class on time. Starting on time is a more meaningful concept than simply beginning instruction when the bell rings. The most important reason is increasing time on task.

The central issue in classroom instruction is time on task. If the teacher gives away the first ten minutes of class, then the students will miss out on instructional activities that could have been completed during that time. In university courses which last two periods, which means two hours, a class is usually 50 minutes per period with a ten-minute break in between. This means that a class has 100 minutes of instructional time. Teachers can easily convert 100 minutes into 100%, so that missing ten minutes is the same as losing 10%. To convey the importance of the first ten minutes, ask students when they go to a movie theater if they like missing the first 10% of a movie. Every minute is needed to get the work done, and the teachers set the agenda. The teacher has the responsibility to start on time.

A: You are late.

B: Sorry teacher. The bus was late.

A: No, you are late. Maybe you should take an earlier bus.

B: OK.

A: What time does this class start?

B: 8:10 AM.

A: Right. How long does your bus ride take?

B: Uh, 30 minutes.

A: What time do you catch the bus?

B: About 7:45.

A: If you catch a 7:45 bus, and your bus is on time, it will arrive about 8:15.

A: This class starts at 8:10, which means you are planning to arrive after the class starts.

B: Sorry, Teacher.

A: Why don't you take an earlier bus?

B: I'm tired.

A: Why are you tired?

B: Because I don't get off work until 11:00 PM.

A: I can see your time management system very clearly.

A: Work late, sleep late, and arrive late for your 8:00 class.

A: Do you see those students sitting in their seats, working on the assignment I just gave them?

B: Yes.

A: I am supposed to be teaching them, not talking to you about your system to cut 10% of this class every Monday morning.

B: Sorry, Teacher.

A: I will take care of you when I have time.

A: The rule is "when you are late, you wait."

A: Please fill out the late student sign-in sheet.

A: You can wait right here until I can check your entry on my Late Student Sign-In Sheet and tell you that you can sit down.

A: I was just about to select a student reader.

A: When student readers are at the front, I can take care of late students, check to see if your textbooks are open to the right page, and make sure everybody is on task.

A: This is called time on task, and it is time for you to get to work.

Lesson 003

Assigning Seats

Teachers need to assign seats, and students should be asked to sit in their assigned seats. One of the many benefits of assigned seats is the ease of taking attendance. With assigned seats, teachers need only check which seats are empty, which is faster than calling names and more accurate than passing around a sign-in sheet. When teachers implement assigned seating, they can use student seat data for numerous classroom management and instructional tasks. Assigned seating reduces an administrative chore in the beginning of each class session that should be spent of English speaking and writing.

In the beginning of a course, teachers should project names and seat numbers. Projecting a seat list can be accompanied by printed copy for use when a late-comer arrives while students are speaking and writing at the front of the room. Teachers should make the late student wait, and avoid interrupting the student language production at the front. Since most students quickly learn their seat numbers and locations, seat number lists and projections are not needed for more than the first couple of classes, though they may also have a brief additional use right after add-drop week ends. Naturally, assigned seats have to be implemented on the first day, and any attempt to introduce seat assignments after the second week of class will surely fail.

Teachers can reinforce seat numbers by assigning biopages and requiring header paper, both of which incorporate both seat number and name. Seat numbers are also essential to make sure every student contributes to the class by going to the front to speak and write. However, for classroom management purposes, names are more important than seat numbers when addressing students. In order to have cordial relations with students, teachers should memorize names. Actually, when the opportunity presents itself, such as when identifying late arrivals (a negative case) or asking student presenters to come to the front (a positive case), teachers use both the student names and seat numbers. When students arrive late, calling them by name and using their seat number is especially effective in getting them to realize that the teacher is keeping track. Likewise, when asking students to go to the front of the classroom and speak, most students want to make sure they get credit for their effort, and it helps all class members to feel comfortable when the teacher keeps track because reluctant students are identified and asked to participate.

The effectiveness of using seat numbers outweighs the reaction of students to the old K-12 system for managing students in classrooms. No other number is more effective for keeping track of students. Student ID numbers are too long and cumbersome. Letting students choose their own seats means that teachers spend an inordinate amount of time matching names and roster numbers. Tracking student arrival and departure in the classroom has many uses, the most important of which is keeping students on task. When seats are assigned in the first five minutes of a new class, the process sends an unmistakable message to the students. The message is that they have to toe the line. Teachers need not be mean about it. Seat numbers are merely a traditional method for teachers to take care of classroom business. Of course, if teachers fail to follow through with the classroom management and instructional techniques that increase student participation, students will quickly sense that this aspect of the class has no value and is not necessary to follow. Therefore, the teacher has to get right to work and start incorporating hands-on teaching techniques.

A: We have assigned seats.

A: If you don't remember your assigned seat number, you can check my list.

A: Let's go. Get into your seats. Time to start.

A: Come on in, and sit in your assigned seats.

B: Where is my seat?

A: Look at the screen. I am displaying a seating plan.

A: Or check that name list on the desk by the door.

B: OK.

A: Find it?

B: Yeah.

A: Thank you for coming on time.

C: Is my seat the same?

A: Check the list or the screen.

A: Everybody has an assigned seat.

A: Excuse me. That seat is not used in the class.

A: Nobody gets to sit in the back row by the window.

A: Are you in this class?

D: Yeah.

A: Check your seat number, and sit in your assigned seat.

A: Time to start.

A: Please review the vocabulary list on page 75, and the vocabulary review for Unit 7 on page 123.

A: Please start your review now.

A: Willy, Seat 7, come on in.

A: You are late.

A: I knew you were late or absent because seat 7 is empty.

A: All I have to do is look at the front row, and I see your empty seat.

A: Please wait.

A: I will be with you soon.

E: OK.

A: Let's see. Where were we before being interrupted by a late student?

A: Oh yes, I was about to select a student to come to the front to read for us.

A: Let me check my contribution checklist.

A: Nelli, seat 4, and Jenny, seat 5.

A: Nelli, you are the reader. Please get the mic.

A: Jenny, you are the computer operator.

A: Please highlight the first line.

A: Everybody, please read silently and follow along as Nikki reads from my lesson plan which is displayed on the screen.

A: Nelli, please start reading line here. Here. See where I am pointing at the screen?

A: Willy, I will be with you in a minute. Remember, if you are late, you wait.

E: OK. What is my seat number?

A: Seat 7.

A: Nelli, please start.

See Appendix 3.1 for a list of assigned seats.

Lesson 004

Introducing Yourself

In the beginning of a class, teachers should tell students what names to use in the class. Teachers should indicate how they like to be addressed, and they should give students a naming system for each other.

Many English classes incorporate English names, but that should not be a requirement. Teachers should encourage students to use whatever name they want. Sometimes a short statement about using your Chinese or English name is necessary, but other ways are just as good. In classes which have a biopage, where the students provide basic name and major information, a series of boxes can work just as well. For example, if the biopage has three boxes for names (English name, pinyin name, and Chinese name), teachers can tell the student that they will be called by whatever name in the top box, including nicknames.

A: James, seat 32, you're earlier than usual. Only five minutes late today.

A: Pick up the new handout and the paper I'm returning. Then sit down.

A: The next person who comes in is late.

A: Turn to page 102 and preview noun clauses while I check textbooks.

A: I can see somebody looking in the door. Please preview noun phrases while I find out who this is.

A: Come in. May I help you?

B: Uhh.

A: Are you in this class?

B: I think so.

A: Is this the first time you have come to this class?

B: Yes.

B: What is your name?

A: Chinese name?

B: Fine. Chinese. English. Any name will do.

B: My name is California.

A: Welcome, California. It seems that I am your English teacher. Please call me Alex.

B: OK.

A: I prefer Alex, but you can call me Guo-hua.

A: Of course, if you need me, you can call me Teacher Alex, or just Teacher, or you can simply say raise your hand to get my attention.

A: There is no need to call me Professor Alex or Professor Hsu.

A: And, I dislike being called Dr. Rath.

A: I don't stand on formality, so Alex will do.

B: OK.

A: Since this is your first time in this class, I would like to point out the 40 students came on time.

A: See them? I'd also like to point out that we are busy.

A: You, however, are putting in your first appearance after missing the first three classes.

A: Therefore, let me introduce you to a phrase you will hear a lot in this class.

A: The phrase is "if you are late, you wait."

B: OK.

A: Please wait right here, and if somebody else shows up late, they can stand in line behind you until I have time to process late students. Got it?

B: OK.

A: Thank you, California. Now, I have to get back to work.

Lesson 005

Discussing Class Time

Discussing class time is a skill. Although students know the posted class times, some students need to be reminded. Of course, an elaborate explanation of class time is unnecessary. Mentioning class time, discussing late arrivals, and talking about missed classes calls attention to it without belaboring the point. For students, review of class time is part of the process of getting them to take their responsibilities seriously.

Teachers should take the opportunity to remind students who fail to take class time seriously when it comes up in conversation. While there are many ways to address the issue, one of the most effective ways to make reference to tardiness and absences is in terms of time on task. Pointing it out by discussing jobs is useful. One analogy is punching a clock at FamilyMart. Teachers can say that students who want to get paid have to put in the time, and punching the clock is a measurement system for the time on task. Language learning, teachers can say, is no different than a part-time job as a clerk. If students want to master a subject and develop a skill, or if they want to make some money, they must put in the hours. Another good analogy is sports. Whether discussing paychecks from a mini-mart or baskets on the court, reminding students about time and the correlation with development highlights the outcome. Gains are made because students put in the time, and attending class is the single most important category of time they must spend.

A: You're late. Come in, and sit in your assigned seat.

B: Thank you, Teacher.

A: You are late. Come in, and sit down.

C: Sorry.

A: When does class start?

C: Class starts at 8:10.

A: Why are you late?

C: Traffic jam.

A: Please be on time to class.

A: OK. Next person.

A: Hildie, seat 52, you are late.

A: You are only a couple of minutes late.

A: If you were any later, I would make you sign in.

A: Class starts at 8:10, and you should be in your seat, with your book open and pen in your hand, by 8:09.

A: Got it?

D: Yeah.

A: We start on time, take breaks on time, and end on time.

A: Who wants to start late and leave early? Raise your hands.

A: A few honest souls. Thank you for raising your hands.

A: Some professors have their ways to take it easy, like cutting the break and letting the class go more than ten minutes early, sometimes more than ten minutes early.

A: One more time. Listen up, and raise your hand if you agree.

A: Who wants to take it easy?

A: Good, no hands.

A: Who wants to start early, skip the break, and stay late? Raise your hands.

A: No hands. Good. I feel the same way.

A: It looks like we agree.

A: We stay for the allotted time, and do the required work.

A: We start on time, take breaks on time, and we end on time.

A: Is that OK with you? That's what I want to do.

A: I call this system time on task, and it will help you improve your skills.

Lesson 006

Discussing Attendance

In terms of time on task, no single activity is more important than attending class. While many students feel a general commitment to attending class, getting the students into the seats is a tough job every day of the semester. Regardless of whether they are more or less responsible about attending class, university students need to be reminded about the importance of attending every class session for foreign language courses. The main reason time on task is so important for language classes is that students are usually unable to find places with the language being used in numerous and varied ways outside school. The immersion in the classroom language environment is an important element in their training to communicate in the foreign language.

A: Everybody must attend class.

B: More than four absences and you are dropped from the course.

A: Any questions?

B: How often will you call roll?

A: Every day. Any other questions?

B: When can I arrive without being marked absent?

A: If you are late more than 15 minutes, you will be counted as absent for the period.

A: If there are no more questions, we will start the lesson.

B: Can I be 10 minutes late without be marked absent?

A: Are you planning to skip the first ten minutes of class?

B: No, I'm just curious.

A: Although I ask late students to sign in, I don't enter minimally late students into the university student records database.

A: The real issue here is student learning.

A: Are you getting this type of intense language immersion anywhere else? I doubt it.

A: The language environment is only one of the reasons for my insistence on arriving on time and being present for the full class.

A: The main reason is time on task.

A: Students need to put in the time to learn a foreign language.

A: If you want to develop a skill such as jogging, you need to get off the sofa and run.

A: Every day you will run a little farther.

A: Students who want to become fluent in a foreign language are like runners preparing for a marathon.

A: They have to run every day.

A: Now, let me ask you something. What time does this class start?

C: Uh... 8:00.

A: No, class starts at 8:10. That is when you have to start working. Got it?

A: In order to learn English, you have to attend class.

A: You can't learn English sleeping late or drinking coffee.

A: You have to attend class, and do the work in class.

A: That is the number one job of English majors.

A: Time on task.

A: More time speaking and writing.

A: The more you speak and write, the better your English will get.

A: Any questions? No? Good. Time to start the lesson.

Lesson 007

Discussing Breaks

Most two-hour classes include a ten-minute break. Breaks are good for everybody, and teachers should take them. Although many teachers work during breaks, talking with students or preparing computer files for use after the break, they are a period of rest compared to direct instruction. For students in a foreign language environment, breaks give them a chance to relax and stop struggling with English. Listening to a foreign language can cause fatigue, and many students are unable to concentrate for long periods of time when required to listen to a foreign language. Breaks are an important part of class, but teachers have to make sure that students return in a timely manner after the break.

The best way to make the class run on time is to use the clock. Watching the clock and starting at the right time is the key. Tell students that the class starts on time, students get breaks on time, and the class ends on time. Following the stated plan is necessary, as students will quickly notice if the teachers does not follow through. The phrase "time to start" is the signal. After signaling the class, teachers have to start the second half of class without hesitation. They need to grab the mic, and start the next activity, or pick up where the activity left off and keep going. When students appear after class has restarted, teachers need to make a quick comment. In the first few minutes after starting, the teacher has to say something about time but not do anything other than get the student on task. When students are five or ten minutes late, teachers should find out the nature of the problem and then respond accordingly. If the student is normally punctual but is ill or uncomfortable, teachers can comment on the student's usually timeliness and remark that this incident is understandable. For recalcitrant students, teachers can make them wait, and after getting the class on task they can go over the class schedule with the waiting student. It is important to determine the reason, and for repeat offenders making a note on the student's biopage is a good reminder to keep an eye out for continued tardiness. While there is no one-size-fits-all response, teachers who generally check out late arrivals will be rewarded with increasing compliance to the regular class schedule.

A: We always take breaks, and we take our break at the time the bell rings.
B: I have to go to the photocopy shop to get my homework.
A: The break is from 9:00 to 9:10.
B: So short.
A: We have to stay on schedule.
B: Can I go get my homework?
A: They call it homework because it is done at home.
A: In other words, you are supposed to finish your homework before class starts.
B: I need to hand in my homework.
A: I don't want you to miss class.
A: If you can't print your homework during break, then print it later.
A: I won't mark it late if you get it to me today.
A: Put it in my box or come to my office and give it to me in person. OK?
B: OK. Can I get my printout now?
A: Yes, as long as you are back when the break is over.
B: I will hurry.
A: Janice, seat 21, I haven't talked to you recently.
A: Let me get my biobook.
A: Can I sit here? Catherine is gone.
C: OK.
A: Where did you learn to speak English?
C: In Taiwan.
A: OK, good. I mean, when did you become fluent in English?
C: In senior high school.
A: Was there somebody who helped? Any exchange student? A friend?
C: No, just the teacher, and I like to watch English movies.
A: Which teacher? The classroom teacher? A cram school teacher?

C: A foreigner at the cram school. He was funny, and we sang a lot of songs.

A: Good to know. Let me make a note in my biobook.

A: Break is over. I have to start class.

A: Good talking to you. Keep up the good work.

C: Thanks.

A: Break is over. Take your seats. Time to start.

A: We are back to writing time with the student writers at the front and the rest of the class writing on the papers I handed out.

A: I will start checking your work in a minute.

A: Paul, you are late. Please wait.

A: En-chi and Anna, I will be with you in a minute. Please finish that line.

A: Paul, why are you late?

D: The breakfast shop was slow.

A: Did you run over to Laya Burger?

D: Yeah.

A: Can you eat before class?

D: No.

A: Can you buy your breakfast before class and eat it in the hallway?

D: Uh... OK.

A: There is no eating in class.

D: I ate in the hall.

A: Well, I guess that means you didn't eat your sandwich in class, but you missed ten minutes to get your food and eat in the hallway.

A: Can you do that?

D: OK.

A: Thank you.

A: Please try to avoid missing class. Now, please take a seat.

Lesson 008

Stating Class Rules

Stating class rules is essential for them to become general knowledge. Teachers should hand out a short summary of a few important rules in the beginning of class. The rules, however, are only the starting point. Actually, students do not respond well to long lists of rules. To keep the rule list short, pick two or three, and state the rules in a short and factual way. For example, "no food, drinks, or phones" is clear and concise. All other areas can be called classroom management, class procedures, ways of doing things, and other less punitive-sounding phrases. For instance, "if you are late, you wait" is not a rule. This phrase is the starting point for the handling of late students. The process is summed up in the catch-phrase, and then the procedure turns to the mechanism for handling late students, called the Late Student Sign-In Sheet. The teacher tells the student to sign in, and the students fills in the boxes. It is not accurate to call this a rule. The purpose of rules is to get things done, and the effort on the process to get them done usually supersedes the rule itself.

The key to making rules work is enforcing them. If the rule states that students should not use phones, then the teacher has to ask students to put away their phones every single time they pop out. It is not necessary for the teacher to be rude or mean about it. The key is consistency. If the teacher says class starts at 8:10, then the teacher can't dash into the room, shouting "I'm here" at 8:20. The teacher will lose all credibility in the eyes of the students. Setting an example is the best way to get students to follow rules. After that, consistent enforcement of the rule is the number two method for getting things done.

A: Tony, seat 14, is that a drink?

A: Please put that drink away.

A: Do I have to repeat the class rule?

B: No.

A: Tony, do you remember the phrase "in the bag or in the hall?"

B: Yes.

A: Tony, put your drink in your bag or in the hall. Which will it be?

B: Sorry, Teacher.

A: I can see that you are putting your drink on the floor under the book rack of your desk.

B: I don't want to spill it.

A: Fine. The best way to avoid spilling a drink is to finish it before class.

A: If I were you, I would put it outside if you are worried about putting an open drink in your knapsack.

B: OK.

A: I want the drink out of the way because I don't want to kick over the drink when I am walking down the aisles of the classroom checking student work.

A: If I spill a drink, then I feel compelled to clean it up.

A: We can't have people tracking milk tea all over the place.

A: However, I would rather be teaching English than mopping floors.

A: If you spill it in your backpack, then it is your responsibility.

A: That is how it works. I spill it. I clean it.

A: You spill it. You clean it. Got it?

B: OK.

A: I don't want to spend a lot of time on drinks.

A: Sugary drinks will rot your teeth and lower your IQ.

A: Thank you, Tony.

A: Let's move on and get to my lesson plan.

A: I write all my lesson plans from scratch, and this one is 1563 words.

A: See here in the bottom of the MS Word window.

A: I wrote it just for you.

A: Before we can start learning new language constructs or practicing English, we have to be ready.

A: If you follow the class process, then you will achieve readiness, and we can start the main activity in this class.

A: Everybody OK with that?

A: First, readiness, second, leaning activities.

A: OK. Time to start the lesson.

See Appendix 8.1 for class rules.

Part II

Preparing Classroom Structures

Lesson 009

Greeting Students

Greeting students by name has numerous benefits. In order to have time to greet students by name, teachers should get to class early and set up before class starts. Greeting students by name, even if just a quick hello while setting up, fosters a feeling of individual attention.

Sometimes classrooms are occupied by another teacher. In this case, teachers have to wait in the hall, and try not to push the departing teacher too much. In these circumstances, give students a quick greeting while they are waiting, but this is not a good time for extended conversation.

After setting up, teachers should talk to students. Greeting, while important, is just the first step. Teachers should have a prepared question to ask every student, and they should make notes, preferably in their biobooks, when important facts are discovered. If, for instance, teachers are asking students what they want to do after graduation, a quick note, such as "career goal: flight attendant," will suffice. The goal of this technique is to learn about students, whether it is directly related to their English ability or not, in order to have the knowledge to individualize instruction at a later time.

A: Good morning. Please come in.

A: Hello, Jim, seat 37.

B: Good morning.

A: Come on into the classroom.

A: Good morning, Eva. Eva... uh.. Seat 19. Right?

C: Right. Hello, Teacher Alex.

A: Please get a copy of the handout.

C: What are we doing today?

A: You will be become a confident and fluent English speaker and master the intricacies of the Queen's English all before 10:00 AM.

C: Seriously, what are we doing?

A: Turn to page 102, and preview the section on noun clauses.

A: Eva, what is your career goal?

C: Uh...

A: After you graduate, what job do you want?

C: I don't know.

A: That's fine. Lots of people are undecided. Any ideas?

C: Maybe business.

A: Business is good. Sales?

C: I don't know.

A: OK. Think about it.

A: Hello everybody.

A: Time to start.

A: Good job coming on time.

A: I am happy everybody is here today.

A: Here comes Matthew. I see him in the hallway.

A: Matthew, seat 8, please come into the classroom.

A: Wait. Grab a handout before you sit down.

A: You're not too late.

A: The next student who comes in will be late and have to wait.

A: Here she comes.

A: Elaine, seat 28, come on in.

A: Please wait

A: Have you finished reviewing the vocabulary?

A: Time to start the quiz. Get out header paper.

Lesson 010

Monitoring Late Arrivals

Two methods can be used to monitor students who arrive late. The first method is to take attendance in the first few minutes of class. The second method is to use a Late Student Sign-In Sheet.

Starting each day with attendance gives students a reason to be in their seats when the first half of class begins. Taking attendance in the second half of class is rarely necessary when all students have to sign in after attendance has been taken. In addition to making a note as to who is absent, taking attendance helps teacher to prepare a greeting for late students which mentions them by name and includes their seat number. They know who is late, and can get ready to say names they stroll in.

Teachers should ask late students sign in on the paper when they arrive. Some days, when the weather is bad, or when other reasons make it understandable that students are late, teachers can wave the late-arrivals in without going through the late student sign-in procedure. However, when students arrive more than ten minutes after the bell, and no external reason will explain their late arrival, it is time to make them wait at the front until they can be processed one at a time.

Teachers should ask students to fill in the Late Student Sign-In Sheet. Students have to enter a line of data on the Late Student Sign-In Sheet, including name (Chinese and English), student ID number, seat number, and arrival time. Teachers should check the line of text on the sign-in sheet, as students can be very sloppy about this requirement, such as skipping the time and the reason.

Naturally, teachers should not spend too much time on the processing of late students, so a phrase, such as "If you are late, you wait" can be employed to make the point that the students in the room get instruction first. At a convenient time, after the teacher has given the students an assignment that they can complete, with some working at the teacher computer and most working at their seats, then time can be spared for checking on the late arrivals. For most students, standing at the front is slightly embarrassing, so after one or two times, they try to avoid this situation, and they start arriving earlier. All but the most recalcitrant get the message, and they make a greater effort to get to the class on time. Plus, data from the late student sign-in page has multiple uses.

A: I hear the bell.

A: Time to take attendance.

A: Ten out of 50 missing, or 20%.

A: Not too bad, but could be better.

A: However, you can say that 80% of the students are in their seats and ready to work.

A: That is good.

A: Don't let your friends tell you it's OK to be late.

A: Being on time and displaying readiness to work is the right choice.

A: Uh oh... I see a member of this class in the hall.

A: OK, OK. Come in. No need to sign in late.

A: Get the handouts at the front.

A: I see an old paper with your name on it over there.

A: Please get your paper and take your seat.

A: The next student who arrives late has to sign in.

A: Open your books to page 129, and review the past tense form of the unreal conditional.

A: I need two writers to come to the front, and everybody has to write two examples.

A: Mike, seat 7, and Mason, seat 12. Please write two sentences.

A: Mike, you go first.

A: Mason start your sentence, and type it up after Mike finishes.

A: Astor, seat 44, you are late.

A: Everybody, get to work.

A: Astor, here is the late sign in sheet.

A: Mike, start your sentence with "if." Look at the example.

A: Astor, what is this text-message-style writing?

B: It's my style.

A: "GDMF bus was late"? Really?

B: It was.

A: OK, but let's avoid swear words.

A: Please use a more formal style of writing.

A: Please rewrite the reason section, and let me see it.

B: OK. Here it is.

A: Fine. Please get the handouts, sit down, and start the writing activity based on the example in the table on page 129.

A: Tim, seat 44, you are late.

C: Sorry.

A: Please wait by the door.

A: I have a maxim for late students.

A: The maxim is "If you're late, you wait."

A: Why are you late?

C: I oversleep.

A: Please use past tense.

A: The correct way to say it is "I overslept."

A: I'm busy. I will be with you when I can take a break from teaching the students who arrived on time.

See Appendix 10.1 for the Late Student Sign-In List.

Lesson 011

Banning Distractions

Teachers should insist that no food, drinks, and phones are allowed during class time. Tell students to put food, drinks, and phones in their book bags or in the hall. Tell them to eat breakfast at home or eat lunch in the cafeteria. Actually, the only effective way to rid a classroom of distractions such as phones, food, and drinks is to ask students to stop every single time such items appear.

Stating a rule is totally ineffective if the teacher fails to follow up with individual requests. Such statements should be polite but firm. Teachers who want to stop students during class from eating, drinking, and browsing the net with their phones need to stop the behavior every time. Actually, asking students to stop will never work if students do not have anything useful or motivating to do after they put away their distractions. For example, students sitting in the back row of a classroom passively listening to a two-hour lecture on a topic which seems irrelevant will never be able to sit silently and motionlessly. Not only do teachers have to provide activities which students can do, but the students need to see the value of the classroom activity. If they think it will help them, then they will give up the low-level distraction of phones, food, and drinks because they will see the overarching value of the teacher's lesson, or at least they will follow the class procedures.

A: Come in. Let's go. Time to start.

A: Sit in your assigned seats.

A: Finish your food.

A: No food and drink in class.

A: Drinks go in the bag or in the hall.

A: That means put the drink in your knapsack or in the hallway.

A: We have work to do.

A: Get out your books.

A: Time to start. Let's go. Time to start class.

A: Please put away phones, food, and drinks.

A: Lori, time to start. Please put away your phone.

A: Dolly, you too. You know the rule on phones.

A: Tommy, finish that sandwich, and take out your trash.

A: I don't want trash under your desk or on the seat next to you.

B: I'm almost finished.

A: Good. Eat fast or put it away, and then get out your book.

A: Tommy, please put that gigantic water bottle in your book bag.

A: You know my rules, so put it in the bag or in the hall.

A: Amy, last time you put an open drink in your backpack it spilled.

A: Please take it outside, so you don't get your book bag wet again.

A: Please do it now. I will wait for you.

A: Jennifer, I can see your phone in your lap.

C: Why do you need a phone?

A: To look up words.

A: Phones are very helpful for vocabulary words, but I have a better idea for you.

A: Use your brain, not your phone.

A: Listen for all the words you don't know, and then write them down.

A: When you get time later in the day, look up the words on your phone.

C: I want to check the spelling.

A: Use your best guess when you write it down, and then check your spelling later.

A: If you do it that way, it will sharpen your spelling.

A: If you always look up a word, and then write it down it doesn't help you sound out words and understand their phonetic quality.

A: Time to start. Get out your textbooks.

A: Let's check the schedule, for today and for the next couple of weeks, and then we will look at the composition on page 116.

A: Judy, Seat 31, I see your phone under your book.

A: Put the phone in your bag.

A: In class, we do not use cell phones.

A: Judy, what are you doing?

D: Someone called me.

A: During the break, text your friend that you are in class.

F: Tommy, seat 46, what are you doing?

C: Checking a vocabulary word.

A: That is a good thing, but you should check it after class.

A: Write down unfamiliar words, and check them at home.

A: Switch off cell phones.

A: Do not set the cell phone to vibrate, or use airplane mode.

A: Now, put away the cell phone.

A: We have spent too much time on phones, and we are here to work on English.

A: The point is that you have to spend time working on English, speaking and writing English that you create and produce.

A: Checking you phone can be helpful, but it is not your work.

A: You need time on task, and the task is speaking and writing.

Lesson 012

Projecting Lesson Plans

Teachers should use MS Word to project their lessons. Given a one-computer classroom with 25-50 seats, it is necessary to use a 24-point font for students in the back row to see. Projecting lesson plans helps students by giving them the chance to read and listen at the same time. It also gives them a sense of where the lesson is going if they read ahead.

Many teachers favor MS PowerPoint, which is a mistake for class activities which emphasize speaking and writing. While MS PowerPoint is fine for lectures, hands-on teaching activities have different requirements, which make PowerPoint less than ideal. The formatting of MS PowerPoint slides emphasizes content, and they are useful for adding multimedia. Projecting with MS Word de-emphasizes content, and favors a flat two-level header structure. All media should be disengaged from MS Word and projected separately. Plus, when students who are assigned jobs need to copy from the teacher's lesson plans to separate notes pages to do their writing work, it is less cumbersome for them.

Naturally, teachers have to write their lesson plans before they are projected. This is the most important benefit of all. By thinking about the lesson ahead of time, the teacher can create a series of activities with a smooth transition and the correct order of activities. This process helps the teacher to develop good lessons as much as it helps the student follow along in class.

A: As you can see, I'm projecting the first couple of lines of my lesson plan.

A: That is the name of the class, and the number of the lesson is here.

A: Here is the date.

A: The first job is to take attendance.

A: The second job is to check the schedule.

A: I project the schedule at the beginning of every class so you can see where we are and where we are going.

A: Can you see how my lesson plan lists all the preliminary activities?

A: Back row students, can you see the screen clearly?

A: Cherry? OK? Rex? Can you see?

A: Cindy, wake up. You can't see if you are sleeping.

A: If you want to know what we are doing, check the screen, and look at my lesson plan.

A: I display my lesson every day.

A: I read the lines of text in my lesson word for word, and students should follow along while I read.

A: You will be able to follow the class if you can comprehend what I am saying or the text I am displaying.

A: I always read the lesson plan slowly and clearly.

A: Sometimes I add additional remarks after I read the lines in the lesson plan.

A: Those additional remarks are often spoken at a faster rate, and additional information is usually added.

A: The additional information is on the same topic as the clear step-by-step lines of text in the lesson, but it often includes more complex description, more difficult vocabulary, and tangential information.

A: Students should try to follow my extemporaneous remarks, but some will find it difficult.

A: If you can't follow along, don't worry.

A: The information in the lesson is sufficient, and covers all the basic content and explanation.

A: Please read the lesson, and follow along.

A: It will help you follow the plans I made for today's class.

See Appendix 12.1 for a class schedule.

Lesson 013

Quieting Down a Class

Teachers need to get the attention of students before starting class. After the bell rings, starting to speak should encourage the class to shift from socializing to instructional activities, but a few students usually keep talking. In the beginning, calling the students by name and pointing at the screen is usually sufficient to stop the conversation. However, some students keep chatting. In such cases, a short request to stop chatting will get them on task.

The most important point here is that students need to pay attention and start the assigned activities. Time on task, whether explicitly acknowledged or not, means that the students are attending to class activities.

A: Time to start the lesson.

A: Everybody, look at the connecting phrases on page 49.

A: Dylan, seat 42, Vincent, seat 43, page 49, please.

A: Thanks.

A: Can the students in the back row hear me?

B: We hear you.

A: Jamie, seat 38, are you almost finished chatting with Sally?

A: Thanks, Jamie, Sally.

A: Jamie, you were on time today. Good job.

A: First, attendance.

A: Second, the schedule.

A: As always, I display the schedule so you can see where we are and where we are going

A: Today is Lesson 4. Nothing is due today.

A: Next week, Bio-02 is due.

A: Coming soon, you will have to submit Oral-01.

A: Joanna, you are late, but only five minutes late. Thanks for waiting at the door.

A: You can sit down.

A: Everybody should be reading and reviewing page 49.

A: Elaine, seat 11, are you done chatting with Jessica, seat 12? Thank you.

A: You have to get ready for a speaking activity, and I don't mean speaking with your friend about where you go for lunch.

A: I need to check textbooks, and then I will pick two readers to help us.

A: Review the material now, so if I pick you as a reader you will be ready.

A: Jennifer, seat 56, and Dolly, seat 57, are you sharing a textbook?

B: Yes.

A: Who forgot to bring a textbook?

B: Dolly.

A: Dolly, you need to bring your textbook to every class.

A: Jennifer and Dolly, please read quietly.

A: Everybody should be reading, getting ready.

A: You should know how our class works by now.

A: You read your textbook, maybe work on an exercise in your textbook to check your understanding.

A: I select two readers and a computer operator.

A: The readers go over the text in the lesson, which explains and repeats the text in the book.

A: I give you a writing assignment, and I pick two student writers.

A: Pardon me, Steven, seat 20, are you using your phone?

C: No.

A: Is that your phone in your lap?

C: Yes.

A: Can it wait until the break? Can you survive without your phone for 50 minutes?

C: OK.

A: Put it away. Thanks.

A: Are we ready to go?

A: Uh oh... I see a late student. Please wait. I am busy getting the class started.

A: Let's go... Time to start working.

A: This is called time on task.

A: If you want to improve your English ability, you have to work on it.

Lesson 014

Checking Textbooks

Students need to bring textbooks every day. In the beginning of each class session, teachers should check to see if all the students have brought their textbooks, and make a note of students without books. Since this requirement is important for helping students learn new material and stay on task, teachers should build the textbook check into the beginning of every lesson.

The first step is to tell the students to open their books and preview a section of a specific page. While they are reading, the teacher can walk around the room and check which students have forgotten to bring their books. To reinforce the class rule, the teacher should say something to the student without the textbook. After asking about the missing book, the teacher should make a note of the student name and seat number.

Beyond checking textbooks, walking up and down the classroom aisles in the beginning of the class has numerous benefits. Teachers can check for food, drinks, and phones. More importantly, teachers can see who is ready, and for students who are not ready they can redirect distracted students to the textbook page. That might mean telling them to open their books, pointing out when they are on the wrong page, and reminding them to get out a writing implement.

When teachers sit up at the front and start talking without putting students on task, they risk losing many students who sporadically listen or totally ignore class activities. The teacher has to give the students a task to complete. Sitting up in the front and talking (whether or not PowerPoint slides are being projected) is not a student-centered activity. It allows students to continue ignoring the teacher or passively following along without being involved.

While the main point of checking is to determine which students have forgotten to bring their books, the following step is to use the textbook, especially in the beginning of the class. Checking textbooks and never using the book is a confusing and directionless activity. Therefore, to give the teacher time to process late arrivals, put wayward students on task, and get students involved in the production of new language, teachers should give the students a job immediately after the class starts which utilizes both the textbook and some individual language production activity, such as writing sentences.

A: We need to start the process of learning the ten structural sentences.

A: Open you textbook, and review the introductory information about composition structure on page 27.

A: While you are reviewing the main terms, I need to check textbooks.

A: OK, OK. Good. Everybody in this row has a textbook.

A: Catherine, seat 35, where is your book?

A: I see it. Please open your textbook to page 27. Thank you.

A: Brian, seat 19. Where is your textbook?

B: I forget.

A: Please use the past tense.

B: I forgot.

A: That is only two words. Please speak in full sentences.

B: Uh.

A: What did you forget?

B: My textbook

A: Please speak in complete sentences.

B: Sorry, Teacher. I forgot my textbook.

A: That is better. Still short but better.

A: Brian, I am going to make a note that you forgot your textbook.

A: Bringing textbooks is one of the four measures which are used to construct my participation grade.

A: Please bring your textbook to class every day. Thank you.

A: Stella, seat 36, please turn to page 27.

A: Is that our textbook?

C: No.

A: Are you studying for another class?

C: I brought the wrong textbook.

A: OK. Nike, seat 37, can you and Stella look at your book together a little bit?

D: OK. No problem.

A: Now that I have finished checking textbooks, we are going to review the main point from page 27, which I typed up and placed in my lesson plan.

A: Find the definition of a supporting sentence in your book.

A: Look at the screen, if you want to see what the definition looks like.

A: Find the definition on page 27, circle it, and write "definition of supporting sentences" in the margin.

A: Allan, seat 18, you should be on page 27, and you need a pen.

A: Allen, what are you supposed to find and circle?

E: Uh...

A: Please say it out loud.

E: Supporting sentence.

A: Good. Please use a complete sentence.

E: I should circle supporting sentence.

A: Close. You should circle the definition of a supporting sentence, and write "definition of supporting sentence" in the margin.

—— Lesson 015 ——

Collecting Student Data

It is easy to overlook the importance of student data. Teachers need both general data such as names and student ID numbers as well as individual notes such as the reasons students are late or miss class. Some information can be easily recorded, such as late arrivals, using a sign-in sheet. Other information such as when students who forgot their textbooks can be collected using a checklist. In all cases, teachers need to build data collection procedures into class time.

Data entry is best completed immediately after class when the events are fresh in the mind of the teacher. The papers (sign-in sheets, checklists, or handwritten notes) should be saved in a folder in case they are needed later. The data entry is most easily accomplished in spreadsheets, and line graphs or other data display techniques can be quickly generated for display in class.

Student data is a necessary part of the individualization that occurs when teachers try to increase the number of speaking and writing activities in class. Teachers need to be able to identify students, starting with seat numbers, setting up activities, keeping track of students that have completed language production, reporting to the class the state of class process, and ultimately grading students. When the teacher knows only a few of the students by name, the majority of students feel little or no accountability. If the students know that they will be called on to go to the front and produce spoken or written language, they feel a sense of responsibility to complete the activities, even if there is no major grade attached to the classroom production of English in routine class performances. In order to make major classroom instructional techniques such as using student readers and writers work properly, teachers need to collect student data and display it for all to see.

A: Please review the grammar box on page 15 while I check the sign-in sheet to see if Rita has properly completed it.

A: Rita, seat 31, please use past tense to describe the reason you are late.

A: Rewrite the reasons sentence on the Late Student Sign-In Sheet, and then wait until I check it again.

A: I have to check textbooks.

A: Jack, seat 47, I don't see a textbook.

B: I forgot my textbook.

A: I am going to write your name down.

A: Ask Morgan, seat 48, if you can share his textbook.

C: It's OK.

A: Morgan, please wait until Jack asks you.

B: Can I share?

C: OK.

A: Rita, let me see your new sentence.

A: Better. Now, pick up the handouts, sit down, and open your book to page 15.

A: As everybody should know, I check late arrival, no textbook, no header paper, and contribution, which means going up to the front and speaking or writing.

A: I check lots of other things too, but these four measures make up your participation grade.

A: I will display my data using your secret codes so it is anonymous after the next composition is returned.

Lesson 016

Making Biopages

Since it is hard for teachers to learn the names of students, one method is to collect individual biopages. To help teachers memorize student names, a photo is essential. A name and photo reference page is very useful for teachers. These biopages work better than the online photos in the student records database. A single-sided A4 paper with information about a student can be called a biopage, which is short for biographical page. In their most basic form, biopages contain a name, a photo, and a seat number. Biopages must include student names in English, pinyin, and Chinese. Student ID number and seat number are also necessary. In addition, biopages should include course name and code number. Optional information might include hometown, senior high school, university major and minor, and career goal, but in the beginning keep the biopage simple.

Teachers who use biopages should consider an incremental approach to giving students the assignment. For Bio-01, assign the header and a photo. For Bio-02, repeat the header structure and photo, and add biographical information at the bottom. For a year-long course, teachers need only one biopage for the second semester. Generally, teachers should assign biopages early in the semester. One use of the biopage is to give students homework which is due on the second day of class. Nothing gets students to pay attention faster that getting a zero on an assignment right away. If the first biopage is due on day two of the class, then the teachers should grade it and get it back to students on day three for maximum effect. However, student seat numbers often change in the first five weeks of a class, due to add/drop and other factors. Therefore, teachers should probably assign biopage two on the fifth day of the course, or any time after seat numbers seem to have been fixed.

Some teachers ask students to submit two paper copies of the two biopages in order to keep one copy for use in a class biobook. The other copy should be graded and returned to students. Students rarely hand in two copies, and dealing with the incomplete collection of biopages can be time-consuming. Another strategy is to collect one paper copy from each student, and then make a photocopy of the set before grading. Some departments will pay for this expense, but many do not consider it an appropriate use of the photocopy budget, which means the teacher pays. In addition, teachers should ask students to upload one digital copy, which can be archived and stored on the teacher's hard drive. If a paper copy is missing, the teacher can print one. Of course, some students fail to submit a paper copy and forget to upload a digital copy. In this case, the teacher should write the name, ID number, and seat number of the student on a piece of scrap paper, which can be used as a marker in the biobook, and it is a convenient place to write notes.

A: You are late. Please wait by the door.

B: OK.

A: Jimmy and Ellen, call me when you finish your sentences on the teacher computer.

A: Everybody else should be writing the two sentences which I just assigned.

A: If you are unsure about how to write it, you can see the sentences being completed by Jimmy and Ellen.

A: I will get back on this job in a minute, as I have a mysterious stranger on our doorstep.

A: Are you in this class?

B: Yes.

A: I don't recognize you.

A: Is this your first time in the class?

B: Yes.

A: Do you realize that this is the third day of the class?

B: Yes.

A: Let me check my biobook for your biopage.

A: Ah ha. You are the missing student who should be sitting in seat 3.

A: I have been wondering about that empty seat.

A: Look at this biobook.

A: I have a page from almost everybody, and all I have for you is a piece of scrap paper with your seat number and ID number.

A: Are you student A105310205?

B: Uh... yes.

A: What is your English name?

B: Clarence.

A: Let me write that down.

A: Now, Clarence, you have to wait here while I teach the students in this classroom.

A: While you are waiting, fill in this Late Student Sign-In Sheet.

A: Your seat number is 3.

A: Write the time, seat, Chinese name, pinyin name, English name, and reason for being late.

A: See how it works?

B: Yeah.

A: Plus, you need to submit a biopage.

A: I can't use this scrap paper all semester.

A: If you want me to help you, then I have to figure out who you are and what type of help you need.

A: At the moment, it looks like you need help coming to class on time.

A: Actually, I mean I have to determine your level of English ability, and get a sense of the areas where you need help.

A: If I can do that, I have a better chance of helping you with the things that you, not just repeating general points that you may or may not have completed.

A: You are not in my Biobook, and in fact you are hardly here at all.

A: Look at these biopages. See how I am getting to know the students.

A: All I know about you is your ID number, and the fact that you have a hard time coming to class.

A: getting to know students takes time, and you have to help.

A: The first step is coming to class, and the second step for you is getting the textbook.

A: After that, I would say completing Bio-01 is the next step.

A: Remember, the rule is "If you are late, you wait."

A: Stand right here. I will be back when I have time.

See Appendix 16.1 for Biopage 01 handout.

See Appendix 16.2 for Biopage 02 handout.

Lesson 017

Making Biobooks

For easy access, teachers should place all the biopages in a folder or notebook. A 60-pocket clearbook is useful, but any three-ring binder or notebook with pockets will do the job. In fact, a set of photocopies held together with a big clip will also work. However, a clearbook, which allows the teacher to slip the paper out the top of the pockets, is most useful for making notes in class.

Teachers should bring biobooks to class every day. The books are useful for regular tasks such as taking attendance, and teachers can make notes on the biopages during individual conversations with students. Biobooks and notes are tools which teachers can use in the classroom and in their offices to keep track of students.

B: Teacher, what are you doing?

A: I am memorizing names.

A: I am using my biobook to help me remember the names of the students in the class.

B: Am I in there?

A: Of course, this biobook contains copies of all the biopages submitted by students last week.

A: I returned your Bio-01 papers today, and you have to edit your Bio-01 biopage based on my suggestions.

A: You have to resubmit an edited biopage, which will be called Bio-02.

A: I will add your new biopage to my biobook.

A: I use my biobooks to help me remember names.

A: Remembering names is the first step of individualization.

A: Do you want me to remember who you are?

B: Yeah.

A: That's what I think too, and most students feel the same way.

A: Most students dislike classes where the feel that the teacher doesn't know and doesn't care who the students are.

A: When students feel disconnected from classes, they don't study very much or learn the material in a deeper way.

A: Many students just slide by without digging into the course content.

A: I also use it to makes notes about students after I chat with them.

A: Watch me practice. I'm going to close my biobook.

A: Joanna, Vanessa, Astor, Stella, Sherry, Mike, Matthew, Jack, Amy, Niki, Vicki, Timmy, and... and ...

A: Uh oh... I forgot her name.

A: When I forget names, then I start flipping pages and reading names and looking at students.

A: I will get it soon.

A: I memorize 150 to 250 student names every year using my biobook.

A: It isn't that hard. It just takes practice.

A: I call it a professional skill, and it is part of my job.

Lesson 018

Updating Biobooks

Busy teachers may find it hard to keep their biobooks up-to-date. During add/drop period, students come and go, and the papers in the biobook need to be adjusted. Students routinely submit their biopages late, sometimes long after the due date. Even papers which are submitted on time contain errors. Students forget their seat numbers, and use the wrong section numbers. Most of the work setting up the biobook occurs in the first few weeks of a semester, and efforts to update the biobook can be heavy through the end of add/drop period.

Once a biobook is compiled, it has many uses. Teachers can bring it to class, and during class sessions it is the best place that they can make notes. Biobooks can be used to write observations, and it is a place to make notes during individual conversations with students. Teachers can collect relevant information about students' personal and vocational interests. For example, making a note on a biopage about the reason students are late can help teachers understand individual behavior. Teachers should interview students about career goals, and enter notes on the biopage. Collecting student information, such as the hand-written notes on biopages, is the foundation of individualization.

A: Are you a student in this class?

B: Yes.

A: You must be confused about the seat assignments, as nobody is assigned to this seat.

B: Last time I sat here.

A: That may be the case, but you missed the last class, and seat assignments changed.

A: What is your seat number?

B: Uh, 29?

A: This class only has 28 students. Maybe you dropped the class or got koukao-ed.

B: Huh?

A: Koukao… it's a Chinese word. I added an -ed on the end to make it past tense.

A: Koukao.

B: Oh, koukao.

A: Right, failed due to excessive absences.

B: I only missed one class.

A: Right, only one so far. By the way, nobody is assigned to this seat.

B: What is my new seat number?

A: Now you are getting the point.

A: You missed class, and you don't know where you sit, which means that I will mark you absent if nobody is sitting in that seat.

A: Do you know how I take attendance?

B: No.

A: I check the seats, and if the seat is empty I mark the student absent.

B: I'm here.

A: So I see. Let me check my biobook.

A: What is your name?

A: Jane.

A: Jane, your new seat is 27.

B: OK.

A: Do you see this page in my biobook?

B: Uh… yes.

A: It's empty. I don't have a biopage from you.

A: You missed class. You don't know your seat number. I didn't even know your name until a few minutes ago.

A: I need to update my biobook. When are you going to give me your biopage?

B: Uh…

A: You missed the first assignment, and your score in this class is 0, z-e-r-o, 0.

A: Is that your system? Skip class, skip homework. Are you an empty page in my book of students?

A: You are already falling behind.

A: Please take this class seriously, and please give me a biopage so I can update my biobook.

Lesson 019

Requiring Header Paper

After completing their biopages, students should convert them to header paper. All header papers should have name, photo, and ID box. Students should print header paper and bring it to class on days when in-class assignments are submitted, such as quizzes and timed-writing exams. Header paper can be used for homework and quizzes.

The main benefit of header paper is that the teacher can quickly determine the identity of the person submitting the work. Many students write a minimal amount of identifying information on their papers, and they often squeeze it into the corners of filled-up pages. Using header paper allows the teacher to immediately determine the identity of the student. A secondary benefit is that it sharpens the word processing ability of students, and it helps them practice following instructions, which in English classes means reading and following English procedures.

A: Take out your header paper, and get ready for me to read the words for the Unit 7 vocabulary quiz.

B: Teacher, I forgot my header paper.

A: Sam, seat 57, no header paper.

B: Sorry, teacher.

A: Use a piece of blank paper, and fill in the information that is in the header part of the header paper.

A: Place the information at the top of the page where the header would be located.

B: Can I use the back side of the last quiz?

A: Yes, but you still have to fill in the information on the backside that is in the header.

A: Peter, do you remember your seat number?

B: Yes.

A: Is that the correct seat number in the header section of your paper.

B: No.

A: Please cross it out, and write in the correct seat number.

A: Tornado, seat 52, good job on your header paper.

C: Thanks.

A: You made all the changes, and you have a better photo.

A: Your header paper is much better.

A: Write down the numbers 1 to 5, and get ready.

A: Are you ready for me to read the five words?

A: I am going to read all five words.

A: After I read the words aloud, you should write them all down.

A: Wait a minute.

A: Sunny, seat 44, what is that half a piece of paper with Eric's face on it?

D: I forgot to bring header paper.

A: Please use a whole piece of paper. Half a piece is easily lost.

A: OK, back to the quiz.

A: After numbering, and after writing the words, then write the definitions, and use the sentence format which I require for all definitions on quizzes.

A: I hope you have finished numbering and are ready for the first word.

See Appendix 19.1 for a sample of Header Paper.
See Appendix 19.2 for Header Paper Formatting Instructions.

Lesson 020

Explaining Homework Procedures

After students develop header paper, they are ready to submit homework. Teachers should explain to students that for every homework assignment they need to upload a digital copy before class and submit a paper copy in class. The purpose of the digital copy is for the teacher's archive. The teacher needs a paper copy in order to have a place to write comments and grades, and as a way to return the evaluation to the students.

Most students need an explanation for homework procedures. In order for teachers to implement procedures with which students are unfamiliar, it is necessary to proceed slowly in the beginning and explain clearly, often more than once. Many students have a very casual approach to producing and submitting homework papers, and many students put a minimal amount of identifying information on their homework. In addition, many homework papers are sloppy and hard to read. Improving the presentation of homework format is a valuable skill, and they are easier for teachers to grade.

A: In this class, students need to follow specific homework submission procedures.

A: First, for each homework assignment, students need to upload a locked and encrypted file.

A: The file name has to include specified information, and you have to give me a secret code which will unlock the files.

A: The document has to include information at the top, called the header, and the name of the assignment.

A: Second, students need to submit a paper copy of the homework assignment in class.

A: I process a lot of papers, so all paper copies have to follow the formatting guidelines.

A: Formatting documents is a valuable skill.

A: Like computer skills, formatting is one of the secondary goals of this class.

A: Reading and following English instruction is another valuable skill, and it is one of the secondary goals of this class.

A: That reminds me of an old joke.

A: Read the instructions. If that doesn't work, follow the instructions.

A: In other words, follow the instructions, and do it the way it is supposed to be done.

A: If you want me to evaluate your work, then you have to follow this system.

A: From the assigned seats to the secret codes, the whole procedure is oriented to connecting the people with the papers, and in the end a grade will pop out.

A: However, if you want to maximize your English language learning in this class, then you have to complete every step in this process.

A: Actually, formatting papers, uploading documents, and following procedures will also help you prepare for employment after graduation.

A: These procedures are not so different than what a person might do in an office job.

A: However, let's not get too carried away with discussing employment skills.

A: The goal in this class is to produce as much spoken and written English as possible.

A: Remember, you have a composition due next week.

A: I want you to use all these procedures and techniques when completing Composition-01.

A: I am looking forward to reading your papers.

See Appendix 20.1 for Composition 01 Assignment.

Lesson 021

Collecting Secret Codes

On the first or second day of a new class, teachers should collect secret codes from students. Another name for secret code is password. Students need to complete a secret code form, which should be passed out by the teacher so a paper record can be checked in the event of discrepancies.

After collecting the secret codes, teachers should enter the information in a spreadsheet. It is best to create a column in a grade spreadsheet for this information, but in the beginning a separate spreadsheet will do while checking the codes written by the students. It takes a while to get the exact sequence of letters and numbers correctly entered in a spreadsheet, as there is often confusion about 1 and l or 0 and O.

Teachers should display an alphabetical list of secret codes (without any other information) to help debug the codes. When there is an obvious problem, most students will catch it at this checkpoint, and it can be corrected easily in the teacher's spreadsheet. However, sometimes the problem is not evident until later when the teacher is trying to open a locked and encrypted document submitted by the student. At this point, the teacher should ask the student to make corrections or clarifications on the secret code form. Students who miss this preliminary phase should be given the secret code form at a later date.

A: Please complete this secret code form.

A: I need a secret code from students for two reasons.

A: First, I require students to upload locked and encrypted files, and I need the secret code to unlock their files.

A: Second, I display grade data in class, and in order to present this personal information for all to see I need to use a secret code as an identifier.

A: The secret code should be four to seven numbers or letters in length.

A: Fill out the form, and write the secret code in the seven boxes at the bottom.

B: Can I use Chinese characters?

A: No, please use only numbers and English letters.

C: Should I write one word in each box?

A: No, only write one letter or number is each box.

D: How many letters or numbers should I use?

A: No more than seven letter or numbers.

A: Anymore questions?

A: I will walk around and pick up the secret code papers.

A: Please give me your paper. Thank you.

A: Thank you. Got it. Thanks.

A: Please don't use your name because it tells everybody that it is you.

A: Please change it now, and then give it to me.

E: OK.

A: Thank you. Good. Pass it over. Thanks.

A: OK. I think I got them all. Did I miss any?

See Appendix 21.1 for Secret Code Handout.

Lesson 022

Describing Online Document Submission

Teachers should explain to students the general procedure for online document submission. First, in the beginning of the class, teachers should tell students to submit online assignments before the day of paper submission. Second, distribute a paper which describes the file name structure and the procedure for uploading documents. Third, give students a quick demonstration of the uploading procedure. Use the projector to display a demonstration of the submission procedure. In the week before a homework assignment is due, especially in the beginning of the semester, it is helpful to remind students to upload before the class when a paper copy is due.

After the reminder about the value of locking and encrypting files, teachers should emphasize the usage of the secret code. One of the two reasons that teachers collect secret codes is so they can unlock student uploads. The other reason is so they can anonymously display student data.

A: Please look at the paper which you picked up when entering the classroom.

A: The paper describes the steps for online submission.

A: After finishing your homework, change the filename.

A: Then lock and encrypt your file.

A: Please use the secret code which you gave me for this course and use it to lock your files.

A: After all, I need to unlock the files, and I can't do that without your secret code.

A: After this preliminary work, you are ready to upload.

A: Over the last few years, I have been using Dropbox for online storage of digital files.

A: Go to my Dropbox account.

A: Please note I said open my account, not open your own Dropbox account.

A: I want you to upload the file to my account, not share the file with me from your account.

A: The website address, account name, and password are listed in section one of the handout.

A: Section two of the handout shows you're the file structure in my Dropbox account.

A: Place your file in the correct folder.

A: Please do not touch the other files that are in the account.

A: When you are finished, log out and close the window.

A: I download files from Dropbox regularly.

A: If you reopen Dropbox, and your file is missing, there is no need to get worried.

A: I have downloaded the file.

A: Please do not send files to me by email.

A: The first time might be difficult, but probably now.

A: Most of the students who are enrolled in this course have been uploading and downloading files for many years.

A: It is easy, and you won't have any problem.

A: If you know how to download a song from the net, you can do it.

A: Pretend it's a song called "I Love Homework" by a singer called comPOSITION.

A: The only hard part is writing the lyrics.

See Appendix 22.1 for Online Submission Information.

Lesson 023

Explaining Paper Security

Teachers should briefly mention the importance of online security by emphasizing that it is unwise to upload documents to the net which are unprotected. Many examples can be used to emphasize this point. Examples can include offline examples such as locking bicycles and online transactions such as digital banking. The reason to focus on the real world examples is to avoid telling them that they might be able to download somebody else's homework and copy it. Naturally, it will occur to the students, so they will see the logic of locking and encrypting uploads without a lot of explanation by the teachers.

After receiving encrypted and locked homework, teachers should open all files using the secret codes. If the teacher is unable to open a file, then it is necessary to check with the student in the following class. Plus, teachers can list students who forgot to upload, and an additional list can be added of students who forgot to lock and encrypt. Students naturally want to avoid being on such lists, so it will give them an extra incentive to upload properly.

A: I don't feel that it is necessary to spend a lot of time on this topic.

A: I want to emphasize that nobody should leave unlocked and unencrypted files lying around the net.

A: I am sure everybody knows that there are hackers that can steal your camera photos if they really want to, especially if you are a famous movie star.

A: Nobody wants the photos of spaghetti at an Italian restaurant, but why make it easy for them to steal your files.

A: How many people here have Line Pay?

A: A few people.

A: OK. How many of you want other people to use your Line Pay account?

A: OK. You see what I mean.

A: In this class, please lock and encrypt all files before submitting them to me using the class Dropbox account.

A: As I'm sure you realize, the reason I collected secret codes is to unlock your files.

A: This is part of paper security. I need it so I can access your papers.

A: It is a bad idea to use the same secret code as your password for your online banking.

A: Plus, it is a bad idea to use your name in your password, as the owner of the document is no longer a secret, even if other people are unable to open the file.

A: I am sure everybody here has experience with passwords, uploading, and downloading.

A: This is just a secondary procedure which is part of this instructional system.

A: It's no big deal, and if you don't do it, you won't lose too many points.

A: Submitting papers online is a good idea because when I am looking for student examples I might pick your paper, and then you will get extra feedback from me.

A: Of course, I won't spend that much time on one paper, but I might select parts of three, four, five, or six papers.

A: Then I will compare the papers, and show different ways of writing, all anonymously, of course, so it is a good idea.

Lesson 024

Requiring Document Filenames

One of the teachers' responsibilities is the processing and grading of student work. This job entails a great deal of paper processing. With the advent of online data processing, teachers need an effective method for handling online submission of gradable items. With this in mind, teachers need to explain file name structure to students, and require that they use this system for all uploads.

Students should be required to use standardized file names for their homework. A filename should have enough information to make the contents clear without opening it. One method for naming files is to includes the course, section, seat, ID number, assignment, and the date. For example, this is a possible filename for an essay in an English composition class: ENG250-01-Seat01-A1083200001-Compo01-101519. That filename is clear enough to help the teacher know who submitted it and what type of document it is.

A: Some semesters I have 150 students, and other semesters I have 250 students.

A: Please think about this for a moment. Think about a piece of homework.

A: Imagine a filename called "Homework-001."

A: What would I do if all 250 students uploaded files named Homework-001, and they were all locked and encrypted?

A: I would have 250 files which I couldn't open, and I would have no way of knowing who uploaded which file.

A: It's sort of like getting 250 papers without names.

A: Now, I want to perform a "What if" test.

A: Look to your left, and think about the paper that person might upload.

A: Now, look to your right, and imagine that student's paper.

A: OK, so far?

A: Now, ask yourself if you want somebody else's score, or do you want your own score?

A: You might say yes, or you might say no, but the point is that it is hard to know if that other person's score would be better than your score.

A: For better or for worse, most people want their own score, and they don't really want somebody else's score, especially if they can't pick the other person.

A: Therefore, you should use my system for naming your files, so you get the benefit of your work.

A: You get your own score.

A: In this class, filenames are composed of course, section, seat, ID number, assignment, and date.

A: That way I can look at the file and know who uploaded it.

A: If I know who uploaded the file, I can open it with the secret code supplied by the student.

A: Look at the filename on the screen.

A: This is the system you should use.

A: Follow the filename format on my handout.

A: The format includes course, section, seat, student ID number, assignment, and date.

A: For example, ENG250-01-Seat01- A108320001-Compo01-101519.

A: Let me explain that name for you.

A: ENG250 is the course, 01 is the section, seat01 is the seat number, A108320001 is the ID number, Compo01 is the assignment, and 101519 is the date.

A: That is a clear filename, and I can tell what's inside by looking at it.

A: Since I get hundreds of files over the year, it is important for student to name their files properly so I can store them and open them when I need to check the contents.

Lesson 025

Demonstrating the Upload Process

Teachers need to have a reliable online document storage site. Many schools have online e-learning systems which teachers can use. Most of those systems have an upload function. However, there are many reasons a teacher might want to use an independent online storage location, such as Dropbox. When teachers have more than one class which will be uploading files, it is necessary to develop a file structure to separate uploads into the correct class sections.

Teachers should demonstrate the online submission process used in class so the students can see the method for uploading files. A demonstration only takes a few minutes. It is useful for students who are unable to visualize the steps after reading the instructions. Select two students. The demonstration only requires one computer operator, but students often get nervous when they are up at the front by themselves. Ask the student to create a new document, and type some text into the file. Then ask the student to lock and encrypt the file. After the file has been prepared, ask the student to start Dropbox and upload the file.

Another reason for having an online storage site is for making back-ups. Of course, teachers need a separate storage site for back-ups, as they should not be stored in a place with open access for students.

A: On the handout, I listed the five folders in my Dropbox account.

A: This class is section 12, and it meets on Mondays from 3:00 to 5:00.

A: Look at my example, and you will see a folder entitled ENG250-12 (Monday 3-5).

A: That is the folder into which you should place your documents.

A: Now, I need two students to do a quick demo for the class.

A: Eva, seat 28, and Kai, seat 29, come on up.

A: Eva gets the computer, and Kai is the consultant on the job.

A: Eva, create a new MSWord document, and type the word "demo" in 48-point letters.

A: Save this document to the notes folder on the D drive.

A: Good. Now, rename the file this way:
ENG250-18-Seat01-A101320001-demo-062219.

A: Now lock and encrypt the file.

A: Good. Now start Dropbox.

A: Open my account. The account name is rattle@mail.shu.edu.tw, which is my school email account.

A: The password is s-u-b-m-i-t, all one word, and all is lowercase letters.

A: Good, you are in.

A: Now click on the folder for this class.

A: Good, almost done.

A: Now, upload the file you just created.

A: There you go. It's easy to upload.

A: The hard part is doing the homework, but don't worry.

A: We will practice a lot in class.

Lesson 026

Collecting Paper Copies in Class

Collecting papers in class is an opportunity to give students a chance to get out of their seats. In addition, it can be used to reinforce the use of header paper for class assignments. This can be done by using an orderly submission procedure.

Teachers can ask students to place papers on the platform in numerical order by seat number. Since the students are using header paper, it will be easy to place the papers in numerical order because the seat number is easily visible in the header section. Check student papers, identify missing papers, and pick up the homework. If time permits, teachers can ask students who didn't submit their homework when they will finish it. Make a note on the daily class notes page for later reference.

A: It's time to collect the Audio-01 homework.

A: I hope you brought your homework.

A: I will review uploads in a minute, but first I want to collect the paper copies of your Audio-01 printout.

A: I need paper copies so I can make comments, offer suggestions for improvement, and write your score down for you.

A: As you remember, in this class students place their papers in numerical order by seat number on the platform.

A: Place the papers with the top facing toward the door in one long line with just the header showing.

A: The paper with seat number 1 is closest to the door, and the last paper, from the student in seat 39, is closest to the window.

A: You can move the papers around to make sure that your paper is properly located in the long row of papers from seat 1 to 39.

A: I want to see the header of every paper.

A: That way I can quickly check who has not submitted the homework.

A: All I do is check... seat 1, seat 2, 3, 4, 5, and so on.

A: You can come up in any order.

A: OK. Let's go. Please submit the paper copy of your Audio-01 file.

See Appendix 26.1 for Audio 01 Assignment.

Lesson 027

Collecting Classroom Data

Data about students should be collected by teachers during classes. Classroom data means aggregate reporting of student behavior and notes on individual instances. Classroom data means quantitative information such as who speaks in front of the class. Individual data is qualitative information about what the students said and how they reacted. This information indicates time on task.

Classroom management information, such as which students arrived late and forgot their textbooks, is relevant information, and when entered into a spreadsheet it is data that can inform teachers about student behavior. Every week, the teacher can collect data in class and enter it into the tracking file after the class. Simple data, such as who is late for class (on-time = 0, late = -1) can be interpreted immediately, and data summaries can be used over the span of the course, from daily talks with students to the construction of participation grades.

Student data has numerous uses. Data can be used when talking to individual students, and it can be displayed during class. Most importantly, if a teacher places a special emphasis on one aspect of a course, collecting data can support that specific curricular or instructional focus. Student data is essential for tracking student speaking and writing in class. In a class where the main goal is to increase student language production, tracking the number of times a student goes to the front of the room to complete a speaking or writing job for all to see is an important indicator. It helps teachers monitor their own effort, it shows students the increased number of language production activities, and it is one of the measures which allow teachers to convert in-class activities to grades.

A: Alice and Elaine, don't talk to the students in the first row.

A: You two are partners, and should consult each other first.

A: Now, please write your new sentences using the vocabulary words in my lesson plan.

A: Everybody else should be writing their new sentences on the vocabulary words on your papers.

A: If you forgot the vocabulary words, then check the list on page 42 for the definitions.

A: You should be writing new three sentences with the vocabulary terms.

A: While you do that, I am going to check textbooks.

A: Plus, I have to take care of the late students who are waiting by the door.

A: As you recall, I am keeping track of students who forget their textbooks and arrive late to class.

A: Remember, I collect data on student behavior.

A: In fact, I collect data on four types of student behavior, and I call these spreadsheets my student tracking files.

A: I also track use of header paper and contribution.

A: Of course, contribution is in a different category than late arrival.

A: I want to make sure that all the students get a chance to stand up on the platform and talk and use the classroom computer to write.

A: These four areas make up the participation grade in this class.

A: The participation score is 10% of the final course grade, so each sub-score is worth 2.5% of the participation score.

A: After every class, I update me late arrival spreadsheet so I can study the arrival time behavior of tardy students.

A: Do you know the word "tardy"?

A: Tardy is an adjective which means delayed beyond the expected time.

A: I ask students to come on time, and I check to see who is late.

A: If I ask for it, I should check to see if you are doing it.

A: In the case of homework, I check to see if you did it.

A: The opposite is telling students to do something and never checking.

A: Sooner or later, students soon realize that the teacher is not going to check, and they probably won't do it.

A: The goal is readiness and time on task.

A: Readiness means that students are ready to get to work.

A: If students arrive late, bring breakfast but not their books, and sit in the back row, checking their phones and having a leisurely meal, this is not a learning behavior.

A: Eating in class prevents students from giving the classwork their full attention.

A: Readiness means they are prepared to work.

A: Time on task means students are working.

A: Right now, that means you should be writing new sentences which demonstrate your ability to use the new vocabulary words in complete and grammatically correct sentences.

A: Alice and Elaine, I only see one sentence on the screen.

A: Please switch so you both get a chance to write a sentence.

A: Let's go everybody. I want to see your sentences when I walk up and down the aisles of the classroom and check your papers.

A: Thomas, seat 25, according to my class coverage tool, you are next.

A: I will be there in a minutes, so finish that sentence.

A: Joanna, seat 35, I will talk to you after checking Thomas's work. Get ready.

A: Everybody, get to work while I record who forgot their books and who is late.

A: Edward, Seat 15, no book.

A: Anybody else forget their book?

A: Jim, Seat 41, let me see that Late Student Sign-In Sheet.

A: OK, please sit down.

A: Alice and Elaine, write your third sentence.

A: If each of you already wrote one, then you can decide who will write the third sentence.

A: You each get a contribution point for the student writer job.

A: Call me when you have finished the third sentence.

A: Don't just stand up there and wait.

A: Duoduo, seat 53, are you sleeping? No sleeping. It is writing time.

A: Thomas, here I come.

See Appendix 27.1 for Student Tracking Data for Late Arrivals.

Lesson 028

Writing Teacher Notes

Writing notes means putting a few words on paper. Noting that a student is late (0 or -1) in a spreadsheet does not explain why. Making descriptive note can explain the reasons behind the patterns recorded in the spreadsheet data.

Teachers can write notes in a variety of places, but it is important to have a central repository for notes about students so the information is easy to find. Teachers can quickly make notes on a clipboard. In addition, photocopies of data collection papers can speed along the process. Teachers can add notes to biopages in biobooks. It is better to jot down a quick note right on the spot than try to remember later. Plus, papers with notes about class can be used as a reference during individual conversations with students.

A: You took a 20-minute break today.
B: Sorry, Teacher.
A: Is that paper in your hand the homework?
B: Yes, I have it now. Can I give it to you?
A: OK, but why didn't you turn in the homework when I collected it earlier.
B: I had to print it, and I was late.
A: Are you telling me that you planned to print the homework during class?
B: No, I planned to print it before class.
A: When?
B: At 8:00.
A: Class starts at 8:10. How would you have enough time to print it?
B: Sorry, Teacher.

A: Do you have a printer at home?

B: No.

A: When did you finish your homework?

B: Last night.

A: In case you forgot, the word homework means work done at home, not during class.

A: It looks like you didn't allow for printing time, and you planned on using class time to print your homework.

A: I am going to make a note about this.

A: You were late to class, and you took a 20-minute break.

A: You didn't submit your homework on time, but it isn't that late.

A: I collected homework at 8:15, and you gave it to me at 9:20.

A: Why do you wait until the last minute?

B: I'm too busy.

A: Is this a time management problem?

B: Yes, Teacher.

A: OK. I will make a note here in my biobook that you need to work on time management.

A: Next time I collect homework I will ask you if you have improved your time management.

A: Now, get back in your seat, and start the classwork.

A: In case you forgot, classwork means work done in class, which you have been missing.

A: The goal here is time on task, and the task right now is writing a paragraph.

B: OK, Teacher.

A: Good. Now, get to work.

——— Lesson 029 ———

Managing Student Data Spreadsheets

Tracking student work, such as the number of times students contribute to class, requires both in-class and after-class procedures. Four types of data are tallied each week using a spreadsheet. The four types of data are (1) late to class, (2) no textbook, (3) no header paper, and (4) contribution. The Late Student Sign-In Sheet is the primary source of data on late arrivals. After collecting quiz papers, the teacher checks the quizzes to see who forgot to use header paper. Teachers should check if everyone has a textbook during the beginning of each class, and should make a note of those who do not have one.

In terms of contribution, when assigning jobs during a speaking or writing activity, it is necessary to keep track of student participation. Asking students to volunteer in class rarely proves useful for getting all the members of the class to participate. The teacher should select students to contribute to classroom activities using a contribution tracking file in order to make sure all students get a chance to practice. Therefore, the teacher needs to record the number of times which the students in the class complete speaking and writing jobs.

Teachers should enter data after classes, and keep their contribution spreadsheets up-to-date. Before class, teachers should print the contribution spreadsheet so they can select students who need to participate during class activities. The teacher can bring the printout to class, and check the printout when picking students to do jobs. Using the contribution checklist means that teachers have a way to get students to help other than volunteers, and it increases the number of times that shy students and those who feel embarrassed at the front have to practice their speaking and writing skills for all to see. An additional benefit to getting the shy and low-level students to demonstrate at the front is the generation of authentic errors that become the source of discussion about how to improve English production. Teachers will find classroom assignments of speaking and writing jobs easier with this type of tracking tool.

Many teachers are uncomfortable selecting students to come to the front to complete activities. Assuming the teacher has a job which is appropriate for the student to complete, small enough to be quickly completed and at the appropriate level for the students in the class, the contribution checklist makes the job of picking students fast and efficient. Actually, for most teachers, the challenge is really choosing a relevant and appropriate instructional activity. Managing the student activities with a data tool is the lesser challenge.

A: According to my records, Iris, Seat 8, has to catch up on her contribution points.
A: Iris, come on up.
A: I need another student to help Iris.
A: Does anybody want to volunteer?
A: Daniel, good for you. You volunteered.
B: Uh... No, I didn't,
A: You raised your hand.
B: I was scratching my ear.
A: OK, you didn't raise your hand very high, but it looked like you were volunteering.
B: Not me.
A: That's too bad. You could do it. No problem.
A: Nobody ever volunteers.
A: It's a good thing I keep records of how many times students contribute to class activities.
A: OK, let me see. Karen, seat 10, please join Iris at the front.
A: Iris, I called you first, so you get the microphone.
A: Karen, you are the computer operator.
A: Please select the first line of text on the screen.
A: Iris, are you ready?

A: Please read the first sentence.

C: Wait a minute.

A: Why?

C: I want to practice.

A: Good idea. You and Karen practice.

A: Karen, you get every other line.

A: Karen, you start as the computer operator, and then you switch.

A: According to the class coverage tool, I was working this row here.

A: Jennifer, seat 14, you are next.

A: Get ready to read the first line for me.

A: I am going to work this row for a couple of minutes, and give Iris and Karen a chance to practice.

Part III

Running Participatory Activities

Lesson 030

Requiring Classroom Contribution

Many students are reluctant to stand at the front and speak in front of their classmates. Some students are scared and seek every possible way to avoid the task. Therefore, teachers need a way to help students overcome their natural desire to avoid standing on the platform and speaking English in front of the whole class. Likewise, students want to avoid letting other people see their English writing. Of course, a few students welcome the attention, and it is necessary for teachers to avoid becoming overly reliant on the few members of the class who constantly volunteer.

Classroom contribution focuses on two aspects of student work in the classroom, speaking and writing. In order to get all the students to participate, a procedure must be in place that makes contribution mandatory. An effective classroom contribution system should not only track participation (defined as speaking and writing for all to see), but also evenly distribute the classroom production of language to all students, including the shy and those lacking confidence.

In addition to having a checklist, or some other means of tracking student contribution, teachers should raise student awareness of this process by discussing it when selecting individuals to contribute to classroom activities. Teachers should regularly remind students that if they have a question then probably 50% of the other students have the same question. Likewise, tell them that if they make an error, then all the other students will benefit from hearing or seeing the error corrected. Authentic examples are closer to the level of student skill than textbook or teacher examples.

Requiring classroom contribution means student readers, writers, and computer operators have to participate. Producing new language for all to see and hear is the underlying idea behind classroom contribution. This process helps students build language production capacity and provides many entertaining moments, some of which helps everybody in the classroom appreciate their progress as they stumble along. At times, the experience is so entertaining that laughter erupts and spontaneous English correction is shouted out, revealing student involvement from many who are passive in other classes.

A: Now that the class is underway, and the obvious aspects of my instructional system are in place, I need to explain the contribution requirement more clearly.

A: Arriving on time, bringing the textbook, and sitting in assigned seats are more about readiness than teaching and learning.

A: Teaching means the instructional system.

A: Curriculum means the content of the class, especially the content in the textbook.

A: To recap, instruction is teaching methods, and curriculum is class content.

A: With this in mind, students sometimes ask how to learn new material and how to improve their English skills.

A: Or they might ask, about ways to raise their TOEIC scores.

A: In language learning classes, practice is essential.

A: Since using a language is more of an art than a science, it is necessary for students to regularly produce bits and pieces in the new language.

A: They have to put the pieces together and evaluate the result.

A: Seeing a fully formed sentence is fine as an example, but asking students to write their own sentences is much more of an authentic learning experience for them.

A: After language production, students need to check to see how they did.

A: The students need to check their work for errors and get feedback.

A: They find out how to produce the same idea or make the same statement without the initial errors.

A: While asking their peers for help is fine for small problems, the nature of getting assistance from a fellow classmate is limited.

A: The teacher has the central role in this regard in providing support, assistance, and direction.

A: The teacher introduces the content to be practiced, and creates the activity where the student produces the bit of language.

A: Then the teachers make suggestions for improvement.

A: In other words, students have to speak and write, and they have to get suggestions for improvement.

A: This process has to be repeated many times, for individual students, small groups, and the whole class.

A: One way to get students to produce language is to ask them to come to the front, and speak into the microphone or write on the computer.

A: If all students are trying to produce something similar, this activity will produce greater benefits.

A: The students at the front get suggestions from the teacher, and the students sitting in the class gain more from the suggestions because they are trying to produce the same type of language construction.

A: Students at the front are not just practicing.

A: They are producing language for everybody to see and hear.

A: Teachers can point out problems with the work, suggest improvements without giving solutions.

A: This process will help students work through the process of correcting their speaking and writing.

A: The members of the class can watch the error student correction process.

A: All this work on the part of the students selected to work at the front contributes to the learning of all the members of the class.

A: The teacher can give contribution points for this extra effort.

A: Even if the points have very little effect on the final grade, students respond to this type of record keeping.

A: In addition, tracking means that the job rotates, and everybody has to contribute.

A: This is fairer, but it also produces a wider variety of student problems and solutions.

A: The overall contribution is greater than getting answers from the same students who frequently volunteer.

A: In addition, it reduces the amount of time the teacher sits at the front and lectures.

A: A little lecture and a few PPT slides are fine.

A: However, two hours of lecture and slides means that students don't get time to produce language.

A: That is why I use a system which I call student readers and student writers.

Lesson 031

Selecting Student Presenters

Teachers should choose student readers and writers using the contribution checklist, and assign them to read aloud using the microphone and write on the computer. To make sure that the student language practice part of the lesson plan is started at the correct time in the class, teachers can place a marker in the lesson. When the lesson plan is projected on the screen, everybody in the class will be able to see the specified activity. A phrase such as "select students" is usually sufficient.

When selecting students, the contribution checklist offers only half the answer. The checklist will indicate the number of times students have completed language production jobs, but it does not unequivocally identify which student is best for any particular job. One determining factor is the degree of difficulty. For easier jobs, many of which are placed in the beginning of a lesson, picking students with less skill is usually better. They have a greater chance of completing a short and easy job. For jobs scheduled later in the class, which are often more complex and designed to integrate several points which have been covered in the preceding exercises, students with greater ability are a better choice. Pairing a low-ability student with a high-ability student usually works out well in the end of class. However, giving two high-ability students the easy jobs in the beginning of a lesson is often a less than satisfactory experience for everybody.

Normally, students should be assigned to a job two or three at a time, which will help them to remain calm. If one student does not know the answer, then maybe another student will. Teachers can assign more than two students. Sometimes, when a reading passage is difficult, it helps the readers for the teacher to assign a third student as a computer operator. This arrangement gives the student readers a chance to switch, and the student who is waiting can prepare for the next sentence. Likewise, if one of the students stumbles over a word or a phrase, help is at hand. Teachers should discourage the students in the front on the platform from reaching out to the front row students. If the two or three students at the front are unable to figure it out within a minute or two, the teacher has to jump in and keep the momentum going.

A: I have to select two students to read some text, and right after that I have to select two students to answer some questions.

A: The two readers have to review these five vocabulary terms, definitions, and examples.

A: After the vocabulary review, I want two different students to answer some questions about five photos.

A: The two students who explain the photos have to use the vocabulary terms in their answers.

A: In other words, they have to identify the connection between the photo and the vocabulary word and the photo, and explain the photo in such a way as to show they understand the term and can use it correctly in a sentence.

A: Let me see…

A: Donny, seat 30, you haven't helped out recently.

A: Otto, seat 39, you definitely need to get up here.

A: Your contribution score is very low since you missed a couple of classes.

A: You two can come up now.

A: I am not selecting a computer operator, as this is a speaking activity.

A: Donny, you get the mic first.

A: Otto, let's see the first photo.

A: Don't peek at the second photo.

A: I'm going to pick two more students to explain the photos, which is a harder job.

A: David, seat 46, you are a guy who likes to talk.

A: You're next. No need to join us at the front now. Please stay seated until I call you.

A: Let me see.

A: Boxer, yeah, Boxer, seat 47. We need your help.

A: We can use a guy like you, but hang on until phase two of this activity.

A: David and Boxer are next.

A: Donny and Otto, your speaking skills are good, but you have to watch your grammar.

A: It's very colloquial, fluid but too informal.

A: I want complete sentences, not just phrases and one word answers.

A: Donny, grab that mic.

A: Otto, highlight the first line. It's not a lot of computer work.

A: You don't have to scroll up or down. OK. You can stop.

A: Donny, please read the highlighted line.

A: Otto, please practice the next line.

A: Get ready to read line 2. OK?

A: Everybody in the class should be reading and listening.

A: OK. Donny, let's go. Start reading aloud for everybody.

See Appendix 31.1 for Contribution Checklist.

Lesson 032

Guiding Student Readers

Changing instructional methods may not result in increased student learning unless the new technique is linked to a broader system that guides the students through the learning process. Regardless of the teaching methodology, this is the job of the teacher. Hands-On English Teaching makes the role of the teacher more explicit. All the classroom management and hands-on methods lead to this point.

Reading aloud helps students in the class to understand the text displayed on the screen. This regular classroom activity introduces the structure of text, including grammar, vocabulary, punctuation, and logic. Student readers should be assigned both short texts, such as definitions of vocabulary words, and long texts, such as descriptive paragraphs. They can read the content that the teacher would have presented in a class using the lecture-PPT format. Student readers should be used in every class.

After selecting students, the teacher should instruct them to read selected passages aloud. Sometimes it is necessary to explain the job assigned to the student readers, and identify the text they need to read. Most of the time, the student reader can see the text and knows that it should be read out loud. After completing this exercise a few times, students will quickly get used to this activity.

While the student readers are speaking, they can be coached for pronunciation. Teachers should not interrupt a reader in the middle of a phrase, as it will interrupt the reader. To begin an interruption, the teacher can raise a hand or finger. The student reader is usually sensitive to the teacher's presence, and will start to slow or stop. When breaking in at the end of a phrase or at a comma, which is a good place because the speaker has to pause, the teacher should identify the word or phrase right away, and explain the problem. Breaking in at the end of the sentence might be better from the listener's point of view, but it often means that the teacher has to remember the problem or problems which have to be remediated. It is easy to forget what the problem was if the speaker goes on for too long. When there is more than one problem, it is important to pick the one that is closest to the language point being taught or practiced.

Students often need help to read the texts aloud. Student readers at the front regularly need the support and assistance of teachers. Teachers can read to model, or they can read to demonstrate speaking skills, such as word and sentence stress. Students need assistance with intonation, and sometimes the need basic pronunciation support. After the teacher demonstrates, it is best to ask the student to repeat. If the student repeats the word and phrase accurately, the activity can move forward. Otherwise, recitation is called for. Asking the student to repeat a word or phrase a couple of times does not stall the class, but this activity should be limited, as the teacher will lose the attention of students. However, for particularly difficult texts, choral recitation is a good option. Choral recitation means that everybody in the class repeats the same text. The teacher can say it, and then ask the speaker to say it, and turn to the class and ask everybody to say it.

Conversation activities are harder to structure. Since so much of conversation is phrases, it is hard to get students to speak in complete sentences, though it has many benefits. To stop a speaker from giving a short answer, the teachers should have a system such as given-new, which requires speakers to repeat the content of the question in the beginning of the answer. In doing so, the listener is reminded about the questions which the speaker is answering. However, this technique requires the speaker to reorder some of the words in the sentence, such as the verbs, to turn the question into a statement. This process requires that the teacher listen carefully to the student's statement, and comment not only on the content but also the grammar and rephrasing. It often takes several tries for a student to get it right.

This type of speaking work takes time, and some teachers will argue that the content is more important. That may be true for some topics, but students need more speaking time in class, and it has to be added by the teacher on a regular basis. This is the heart of the method. Students practice, they get corrected, and they practice again.

A: We are now going to look at examples of if-clauses.

A: Bobby, seat 55, and June, seat 41, time to read aloud.

A: June gets the mic.

A: Look at the box with the four examples of if-causes.

A: June, start by reading the first sentence in the box.

A: This is a general if-cause.

B: If it is too hot... we will turn ... on the air conditioner.

A: June, you are pausing too long after the comma.

A: You are also pausing too long in the middle of the phrasal verb "turn on."

A: Please read the sentence again.

B: If it is too hot, we will turn on the AIR CONditioner.

A: You are placing too much stress on "air."

A: Much better, but you are not giving the word "conditioner" the proper word stress.

A: The word "conditioner" gets word stress on the second syllable.

A: Say it this way... conDItioner.

B: CONditioner.

A: No, conDItioner. Again.

B: Bobby, how do you say "air conditioner"?

C: AC.

A: Funny. That is probably how you say it in real life, but we are practicing speaking skills.

A: Everybody, say air conditioner.

D: Air conditioner.

A: Good.

A: June, please read the sentence one more time.

B: If it is too hot, we will turn on the air conditioner.

A: OK. You got it. Bobby. Your turn.

A: June, you get the computer.

A: Ow! The mic noise, that rattling of the mic hurts my head.

A: June, remember to turn off the mic before handing it to somebody.

A: Mic skills 101. Remember? Turn off the mic, lower it from the speaking position, and then pass it.

A: Bobby, read the second if-clause example in the box.

A: Remember word stress. Remember mic skills. Remember eye contact.

A: June highlight the general conditional with the mouse.

A: Select that line of text so we all know what we are practicing.

A: Bobby, are you ready?

C: Yeah.

A: No, you aren't. You are standing next to June over by the windows.

A: Please stand front and center on the platform.

A: Bobby, I want you to read the future if-cause.

A: Are you ready?

B: Ready.

A: OK. Read the second example.

Lesson 033

Guiding Student Writers

The benefits of incorporating student writers into classes are numerous. The first benefit is that it frees the teachers from standing at the front. When the student writers are occupying the classroom computer, it gives the teacher time to work the room. The second benefit of incorporating student writers is students sitting in the class can see an incomplete but growing line of text on the screen, and it will give them a place to start if they are unable to find the words. The third benefit is that student writers make errors that are common to many students in the class, and many teachers find it difficult, if not impossible, to generate authentic errors for instructional purposes. The fourth benefit is that members of the class can watch the student writers grapple with the errors and try to fix them. A fifth benefit, but not one that is regularly exercised, is that students who start compositions in class that are assigned as homework can take their rough draft, and they can use it later when they are writing their first full draft at home.

While the work of student writers can provide additional models for the whole class, much of the student work is full of errors, and it is probably not best to suggest that it be used as a model. However, when paragraph writing homework is assigned, the work of student writers in class who are given the same assignment as a warm-up activity gives students a place to start, but students should be advised that it needs work and should not be used without improvements.

Teachers should select two students to write the assigned sentences at the teacher computer, and everyone should write the same sentences on writing paper. In the beginning, switch back and forth between the student writers and the class to make sure everybody is on task. After the majority of the students are on task, the teacher should check the initial work of the student writers. Since many get off to a bad start, teachers should give them a little direct instruction to make sure their work is close to the assigned topic. After the student writers are coached and redirected, the teacher should use the class coverage tool to determine which students are next for seat-by-seat review. The teacher should work the selected row with the goal of checking at least one sentence for every student, and making one comment based on the main point being taught. Some writing errors related to the main point are easy to identify, and many people make the same error. Repeat the correction to each individual student using the wording in their sentence as a point of reference.

While working the room, the teacher needs to keep an eye on the student writers. Calling out to them, and asking for a progress report ("done yet?") is good, but it is also necessary for the teacher to scan the text on the screen. If the student writers get sidetracked, the teacher needs to redirect them, either with a quick comment from the seating area or by working with them at the front.

When making comments about the text on the screen, the teacher should stand on the platform and point to the text on the screen, not work with the student writers huddled around the teacher computer where other students are unable to see or hear. When the student writers finish, address the whole class when speaking. In addition, address the student writer who wrote the text being discussed, and make sure that the actual writer is the one making the corrections, which means that the student writers have to switch positions when the teacher moves from the work of one to the other. The teacher should always start by commenting on the text which matches the main point of the exercise, and teachers should try to remember which points have been covered so as to avoid being repetitious. However, some problems, such as informal writing errors, need to be regularly discussed, as the students usually write like they talk. Helping them write in a more formal style is one of the many tasks which have to be addressed in these coaching sessions.

A: I hope everybody has finished working on their paragraphs about the school uniform issue.

A: The two student writers have finished.

A: Good job, Ellie and Isabel. I see you have a well-developed five-sentence paragraph.

A: Let's start with the topic sentence.

A: Who wrote it?

B: Me.

A: Ellie, grab the keyboard.

A: The topic sentence has an issue but no position.

A: Remember the requirements for a topic sentence in an argument paragraph.

A: The writer has to identify both the issue and the position.

A: Ellie, use the background color function, and select the issue being addressed in the sentence with yellow background color.

A: Good. You have an example in the sentence.

A: The example should be later in the paragraph.

A: Highlight the example with the neon green background color.

A: Can everybody see?

A: Look at the two parts of the sentence which are highlighted with two colors, one yellow and one green.

A: This is the issue in yellow, but the position is missing.

A: This is an example in green, but it should be deleted.

A: Now, Ellie, I want you and Isabel to fix the topic sentence.

A: Delete the example, and add a general position.

A: Just edit that one sentence.

A: I am going to check two more student papers.

A: Call me when you are finished.

A: Let me check my class coverage tool.

A: Where was I?

A: Ahh... Patricia, seat 42, you are next. I bet you thought you escaped.

A: Get ready. I am going to check your paper next.

A: Are you done yet?

B: No.

A: Finish it up.

A: I am going to check Jessica's sentence, and I will be right back.

A: Get it done right now.

A: Jessica, seat 32, "you" is an informal writing error.

A: Use the plural noun "students" in your sentence.

A: Isabel, I am sorry to say that you have two informal writing errors in the sentence which is being displayed on the screen.

A: Please select the word "can't" and use the background color function to highlight it with the yellow.

A: Good. Now highlight the word "you."

A: Give it yellow since are using it as an error color.

A: You are breaking the first two rules on the formal writing paper which I handed you.

A: First, avoid contractions.

A: Second, avoid first and second person.

A: That is how people talk, and we are trying to develop a more formal English writing style in this class.

A: Wait, wait, uncontracting "can't" to "cannot" is a change which rarely improves a sentence.

A: Maybe you should try "is unable to" or another verb phrase.

A: Please change both words now.

C: Should I use "one" in the sentence?

A: No, too stiff. People avoid that word.

A: Try using a plural noun such as students or people to name the people which you are talking about.

A: That's better.

A: After making those changes, check the sentence to see if anything else needs to be adjusted.

A: I will be right back after I check a paper or two.

A: Patricia, I'm coming back. Are you ready?

A: Please change the verb. You changed the subject, so you have to change the verb.

A: Everybody needs to finish their sentences, and get ready to review the work by the student writers.

A: I want to start my review of the work by the student writers next. Get ready.

Lesson 034

Guiding Student Computer Operators

Another job which needs to be assigned during student reading and speaking activities is computer operator. Students who are writing rarely need a separate computer operator. On the other hand, student readers definitely benefit from having a computer operator. When students are reading aloud, it helps to have the computer operator follow along by highlighting the words and sentences. This helps the student readers as well as the members of the class.

The basic job of computer operator is highlighting text. To highlight a word or phrase, select the text with the cursor, which temporarily turns it grey. It is best to avoid using the background color function during a simple reading activity. Readers move quickly from line to line, and there is no need for reformatting the text.

Teachers who use digital media can employ computer operators for other jobs, such as looking up words on the net or checking on grammar and usage. In such cases, the student completes the search, and copies the relevant text, which is later pasted in the lesson or in a notes file. Cutting and pasting text is also a regular job, especially during writing assignments.

For students, a general benefit from this experience is improving their ability of listening and following instructions. This skill is especially important after students graduate and find employment. As the English-speaking person in a company or a department, the English major is often told to help the English-speaking foreigners with computer presentations. However, the listening comprehension skills which result from following the teacher's instructions can work in many areas.

If the computer operator is having trouble either performing the job, or following along, remediation is necessary. The teacher should ask the computer operator to follow the reader, highlighting what is being read. If the computer operator is moving text around, jumping around the page, or highlighting the wrong text, then the teacher should intervene. This type the display will distract the students trying to read the text aloud and the students who are listening.

No matter what job the students at the front have been assigned, even the least demanding job of computer operator, the goal is to change the instructional method, and increase student learning. The computer operator job, like student readers and writers, is linked to a broader system that challenges the students to undertake the learning process.

A: I need a reader and a computer operator.

A: Jason, seat 41, according to my list, you need to get up there and earn a contribution point.

A: Coco, seat 43, please help Jason. You are the computer operator.

A: Coco, do you remember the technique for highlighting a line of text.

B: Uh...

A: You place the cursor in the left margin, and use the right-pointing arrow.

A: Just click once, and the line is highlighted.

A: No, don't click and drag. Just click once.

A: Good... you got it.

A: Jason, start reading.

A: We are still working on the school uniform essay.

B: Individualism is a fundamental part of society in many countries.

A: Jason you are reading in a monotone voice.

A: You are placing the same emphasis on every syllable and every word.

A: This is what it sounds like...

A: In-di-vi-du-al-ism-is-a-fun-da-men-tal-part

A: You need to emphasize some sounds more than others, and you need to group words together.

A: Let's start with word stress.

A: Coco, look up the word "individualism" on the net, and check the word stress.

A: Good, that's it. The emphasis in "individualism" is on the VI sound.

A: Jason, say the word.

B: Individualism.

A: OK, repeat the word with a stronger stress.

B: IndiVIdualism.

A: Coco, select the word, and make it bigger.

A: Everybody, say the word "individualism" with the correct word stress.

C: Individualism.

A: Coco, please look up the word "fundamental."

A: Jason, how do you say "fundamental" with the correct word stress?

B: FundaMENtal.

A: Everybody, say the word fundamental with the correct word stress.

C: Fundamental.

A: OK, now, start over.

A: Read the whole sentence, and don't forget the other words which get word stress.

B: The same sentence?

A: Yes, the same sentence. You need to practice.

A: Coco, please highlight the sentence.

A: OK, again.

Lesson 035

Writing Lesson Plans

Teachers need to write lesson plans for every class. Like all teachers, those who lecture a lot and do a minimum of class activities to have plan their lessons, even if they if does not feature speaking and writing activities. Actually, developing a set of PowerPoint slides, all of which feature content, is probably easier than creating an interactive lesson, especially one where students are doing different activities at the same time. Of course, content knowledge requires significant study by the teachers, and the creation of a smoothly flowing PPT is not easy, but it is a different type of class, and one that does not require the juggling of numerous instructional methods and impromptu analysis of student language production by teachers. Experienced teachers can go into a class without much more than this teach for two hours. More developed lesson plans require preparation of handouts and lecture notes, but they also require teachers to think through the classroom interaction. However, teachers who are trying to incorporate new student speaking and writing activities need to work out the details of the in-class activities ahead of time.

For classes which emphasize increased speaking and writing activities, the description of the class process in the lesson plan helps students. Many students are unfamiliar with class methods which require greater participation. They are used to sitting and listening, so they need assistance with this method, especially in the beginning. Displaying the lesson plan is an essential part of the process.

Some teachers display traditional lesson plans, which are typically one page with numbered curriculum points. While these one-page summaries may be concise descriptions of content, projecting them in class rarely helps students. Projection of content, meaning a fuller description, not just a bulleted list of topics, is the traditional teacher system for designing and developing PPT slides. On the other hand, projecting a description of the content and the steps involved in an activity gives students a direction to follow. No matter what age level, projecting the basic description of the class activity is helpful for students.

While it is practically impossible to write a script for every minute of class, the more text that can be projected the better. There are two reasons why this is useful. First, writing helps the teacher think through the curriculum and instruction in each class. Likewise, it creates a situation where the teacher needs to concisely describe each activity for the students. Second, students can read and listen at the same time when the teacher explains an activity or the specified content. When the activity is complex, a written explanation helps the listener get the meaning and follow along.

A: Grammar is so difficult, but so important.

A: Now we start a grammar activity.

A: Turn to page 101, and review the grammar box.

A: The box is an introduction to the infinitive of purpose.

A: The summary in my lesson displayed on the screen is the same as your textbook.

A: My examples are a mix of sentences.

A: Here I retyped the textbook example, and this one is a new sentence, which I wrote.

A: This is the main point: An infinitive can be used to express a purpose.

A: This is the textbook example: I scrolled down to read the text. (=because I wanted to read the text.)

A: Did you notice the little box in the top right corner of page 101?

A: It says that people can also express purpose with "in order to" and "for."

A: More information can be found in the Grammar Booster on page 139.

A: Now, we are going to complete a writing activity.

A: I need two student writers.

A: Michael, seat 27, and Sammi, seat 29.

A: Everybody has to write three sentences.

A: Michael, you write the first sentence.

A: The topic of the sentences is computers since we are currently working on Unit 9, Living in Cyberspace.

A: Follow the steps outlined in my lesson plan.

A: Write the sentence.

A: Draw a box around the infinitive of purpose.

A: Michael, are you going to start?

B: Yes.

A: Sammi, think about your sentence.

A: I am starting on this row, right here.

A: I want to see some sentences.

A: Are you clear about my lesson plan?

A: First, a reader reviews the topic.

A: Second, we practice, either by speaking or writing.

A: Third, I offer suggestions for improvement.

A: That is the basic lesson, so let's get to work.

See Appendix 35.1 for Lesson Plan Sample.

Lesson 036

Selecting Textbook Activities

Teachers need to determine the parts of a textbook to be used in class. A major goal such as increasing speaking and writing guides the development of lessons and the selection of textbook content and activities. No matter what exercises are selected, lesson plans should be constructed so as to facilitate the use of student readers and writers. Likewise, lesson plans should be organized so as to reduce the amount of lecture and the avoid over-reliance on PPT slides. As a result, writing lesson plans is a balancing act that requires a focus on both content and student production of spoken and written English.

Given the limited amount of time in a course, parts of a textbook have to be skipped. In the beginning of a unit, teachers can help students by identifying the relevant sections and specifying the most important pages. Once that content is presented to the students, teachers need to keep it in mind as they run textbook practice activities and evaluation exercises. This alignment of content, activities, and assessment must be fairly clear and relatively focused, and the role of the speaking and writing activities should be to help the students practice the content. Naturally, all additional speaking and writing, besides the part which focuses directly on the content, contributes to student learning.

A: Look at the two-page spread on pages 100-101.
Do you remember the term "two-page spread"?

A: On page 100, the authors placed a conversation model, which you may refer to later if you need an example.

A: Under the conversation model is a vocabulary section.

A: A lot of this vocabulary is too easy.

A: You already know so many English computer words, and these are very easy words.

A: Phrases such as "upload file" are commonplace.

A: You should scan the vocab just to check, as there might be a few which you don't know, but it is not a job for this class activity.

A: Under the vocab is a listening activity, but since the vocab is too easy, we are going to skip that listening exercise.

A: I want you to work with the grammar in the box and the conversation activator.

A: This way you have to use the vocab and grammar in a new conversation.

A: You have to concentrate on two of the activities on pages 100-101, and if need be you can refer to other parts for help.

A: The main idea is to practice the grammar in the content of a new conversation.

A: On the top of the right side is the grammar activity which we just finished.

A: Below the grammar box is a practice activity, and you should complete that one at home.

A: We just finished a writing and reading activity which incorporated the grammar point.

A: Now, we are going to complete the conversation activator lesson on the bottom right

A: It incorporates content from the conversation model, the vocabulary words, and the grammar structures.

A: If you are trying to figure out the conversation activator, check the conversation model for an example.

A: I selected a new topic for the conversation activity so you have to think up new lines.

A: I will select student writers, and now everybody should start writing.

A: Let's get to work.

Lesson 037

Incorporating Speaking and Writing

When the focus of a class is on language production, especially speaking and writing, students need to be helped because they are unaccustomed to this level of activity. Teachers need to explain topics such as pronunciation. Some textbooks have pronunciation content, but the teacher needs to present an overarching view of the integration of content with speaking and listening activities.

Teachers should indicate which content can be found in the textbook, and what material is new and has been added. While supplementary content can be useful, the range of topics which can be added is immense, and new additions quickly move into new areas not immediately related to the textbook. While teachers regularly add original content that is not directly related to the primary curriculum goals, they must keep in mind that adding new material means more lecture time. Teachers should be adding more activities that feature student production of language, which means they have to focus their supplementary activities to fit in more practice and application exercises.

This type of class requires interplay between the students at the front and the rest of the class. It is relatively easy for teachers to keep track of the student readers and writers at the front. On the other hand, working the room and systematically talking to as many students as possible given the available time requires a new approach. Teachers need a way to keep track of the students who have been helped and the students who have not yet gotten personal assistance. One way to keep track is to use a class coverage tool.

A class coverage tool is a seat plan and checklist. Teachers can use it when working the room. As they go up or down a row, teachers can check off who they have helped.

When the students at the front are in need of assistance, teachers can leave the seating area in the classroom without forgetting where they were. Therefore, picking up where they left off is easy. The class coverage tool is useful for large classes because the teacher can start over in the correct location in the following class. This technique helps to the teacher balance the coaching of the students at the front with the assistance to the students in the seats.

A: Many teachers start with the textbook, but not us.

A: In this class, we start with the goal of increasing the amount of speaking and writing that students complete in class.

A: For teachers and students to do their job quickly and efficiently, we use textbooks to guide us in terms of general content.

A: Textbooks present well-developed activities that are part of a larger scope and sequence plan that coordinates many aspects of teaching.

A: Naturally, we don't start on page one and do every single exercise from the first page to the last page.

A: We select the material in the textbook we want to use, and check if it is the right level of difficulty.

A: Teachers present the selected content to students, which means review the content in the book and on the screen (or chalkboard).

A: After presenting the content, teachers assign practice activities.

A: In this class, a major emphasis is placed on speaking and writing during the practice activities.

A: When teachers add supplementary content and activities, it is usually connected to the textbook content.

A: In this class, with its emphasis on speaking, one possible area for supplementary activities is pronunciation.

A: Our textbook has a small pronunciation section in the appendix, and the classroom speaking activities build on that part of the book.

A: The point is more speaking activities for students.

A: The same process occurs when adding supplementary writing activities.

A: The additional writing activities are based on the Grammar Booster of the appendix, which has a small section on composition.

A: On one of the pages in the composition section, the textbook mentions common sentence structure problems.

A: The two problems that are identified in the appendix are comma splices and sentence fragments.

A: Therefore, when we complete special writing activities which supplement the textbook, we build on this part of the book.

A: All of these choices are based on the teacher's plan for the class in view of the curriculum goals.

A: The major goal is to increase the amount of time students are speaking and writing in class, and in homework, too.

A: That is how and why the additional speaking and writing activities are incorporated in this class.

A: While I am working the room, I use a class coverage tool so I can work with students individually while the students at the front do their jobs.

A: On my clipboard is the class coverage tool, and I can see who I am talking to when I check off a seat, which is a benefit of assigned seats.

A: Let me demonstrate.

A: Seat 1, right here on my class coverage tool.

A: As I can see, Momo is sitting in seat 1. Hello, Momo.

B: Hello, Teacher.

A: Are you ready to answer a question and use the language point in your answer?

B: Yes.

A: Good. Let me make a check mark on my class coverage tool.

A: Everybody, do you see how easy it is?

A: Now, student writers at the front, get to work.

A: Everybody else, start working on your paper.

A: Let's go.

See Appendix 37.1 for Class Coverage Tool.

Lesson 038

Introducing Mispronunciation

Speaking English requires an understanding of phonetics and pronunciation techniques. Common pronunciation techniques include word stress, sound reduction, unstressed vowels, sentence stress, micropauses, and intonation. There are many ways to help students with speaking, but no matter which way is chosen, teachers need to add to oral language activities in classes.

Pronunciation is a distinctive way of talking, which is often associated with a place or group of people. While many teachers they want students to speak clearly and accurately, using a normal speaking speed is an equally good goal. Regardless of the type of instruction, students want more speaking activities, and the activities need a focus. The most common focus of classroom speaking activities is content, but this should only be the starting point for coaching students during speaking activities.

In the past, people usually believed there was a right or wrong way to pronounce words and phrases, and the goal was to sound like a native speaker of English. In recent years, the standard has shifted to effective communication. As a result of this new perspective, pronunciation now largely focuses on whether the spoken language is unintelligible to the listener. As such, the goal of pronunciation is to be understood by listeners. Teachers should explain this general concept in class. Any overview needs to include mispronunciation as it relates to effective communication.

A: Cecilia, seat 19, please come to the front.

A: What is your name?

B: Cecilia.

A: Please say it this way, "My name is Cecilia."

B: Cecilia.

A: I mean, please answer with a complete sentence.

B: My name is Cecilia.

A: I wouldn't pronounce her name the way she does, but a name is a personal proper noun and can be pronounced the way she likes it.

A: If someone says you are mispronouncing your name, you can say that is the way I pronounce it.

A: As you probably realize, there is more than one way to pronounce your name.

B: Really?

A; You are pronouncing your name with the emphasis on the first syllable.

A: Another way to pronounce your name is with the word stress on the second syllable.

A: Listen, CE-cil-i-a, ce-SEE-li-a.

A: I never heard anybody pronounce it this way, ce-cil-EE-a.

A: If somebody was calling your name, calling loudly for you, it might sound like this, CE-cil-I-AAAA!

A: Each way to say your name has a different sound, depending on which syllable is emphasized.

A: First, say ce-SEE-li-a.

B: ce-SEE-li-a.

A: Now you say the name the way you always pronounce it.

B: CE-cil-i-a.

A: Thank you. You may sit down.

A: That was an example of pronunciation, but I would hesitate to call it mispronunciation, as names are personal pronouns.

A: Now, I want to explain mispronunciation.

A: Mispronunciation means saying something that people don't understand.

A: I want to demonstrate this problem with a true story.

A: One afternoon, a Taiwanese student met some exchange students from France.

A: One of the French students said, "Do you want to go to make donuts?"

A: The Taiwanese student thought it would be fun, so she joined the group.

A: After walking for a while, they went into a McDonald's.

A: The Taiwanese student asked, "When are we going to make donuts?"

A: A French student said, "This is it. Haven't you heard of Make Donuts?"

A: What is the point of this story?

A: Maggie, seat 30. You're next.

A: What do you think?

C: Not any donuts.

A: Close. Your answer is an unclear statement, but I think you understand.

A: Why aren't there any donuts?

C: Because she didn't understand.

A: Good. I could spend some time helping you rephrase your answer, but we have to keep moving.

A: The point is that mispronouncing words can cause confusion.

A: The Taiwanese student didn't get any donuts because she was unable to understand the French student, or you could say the French student mispronounced the name of the restaurant.

A: Mispronunciation means the listener doesn't understand.

A: It doesn't have to do with sounding like an American, or any other type of English speaker.

A: The question of effective communication turns on comprehension.

A: In the old days, the oral language of students was compared to a standard to a particular accent.

A: Now, with many different forms of English being used all over the world, the goal is clear communication.

A: When adding vocabulary, grammar, common phrases, and other parts of language expression, effective communication and the resulting comprehension is a challenge.

Lesson 039

Explaining Mispronunciation

In classes with speaking activities, the teacher has to decide how to handle mispronunciation. After explaining that the goal is clear communication, teachers can get students to mispronounce some words so as to have examples. While it can be tricky to get students to mispronounce words when needed, asking students to say words that are commonly said wrong is a good way to generate some authentic student errors.

In terms of pronunciation, some teachers compare prescriptive and descriptive methods. Many aspects of linguistics are conflicted about this point. Prescription means of rules explaining how pronunciation should be handled should be done. By comparison, description means explanation of how words and phrases are actually spoken. Since pronunciation means the ways word and phrases are spoken, the term can refer to agreed-upon sounds in a specific dialect, termed correct pronunciation, or the way a person speaks. In language classes, teachers need a framework to discuss pronunciation. The concept of effective communication sidesteps this debate, though it might be useful to explain the issue to students in classes with speaking activities.

A: Mickey, seat 52, your turn.

A: Please come to the front, and read this word.

B: miss-pron-noun-ci-a-tion.

A: OK, now read this sentence.

B: Pron-noun-ci-a-tion is an a-greed u-pon see-quence of sounds when spee-king.

A: Hmm... Several problems could be discussed, but I want to mention on one major issue.

A: Speakers of English need to avoid the monotone, the one syllable at a time way of speaking.

A: Now, say this word: h-e-r-b-s.

B: H-erbs, her-bs...

A: Say it again without the hh sound.

B: erbs.

A: Thank you, Mickey. You can sit down.

A: We need to talk about pronunciation and mispronunciation.

A: Speaking clearly may or may not refer to pronunciation.

A: Some terms such as articulation means to state words clearly and distinctly.

A: Accent, on the other hand, means speaking in a way often associated with a particular group of people.

A: I need two student readers to help us.

A: According to my contribution checklist, we haven't heard from Nini, seat 31, and Charat, seat 32, recently.

A: Come to the front, and read this list of words for us.

A: Nini, start with these words.

B: pronunciation
pronounce
pronounces
pronouncing
pronounced

A: Nini, you are mispronouncing the word "pronunciation."

A: You are saying the noun like the verb.

A: The noun is pro-NUN-ciation, not pro-NOUNCE-iation.

A: Please repeat these two words.

B: pronounce
pronunciation

A: Good. You said it correctly this time.

A: Charat, please read the next set of words.

C: mispronunciation
mispronounce
mispronounces

mispronouncing

A: Good. You got it.

A: Nini, please read some more for us.

B: enunciate

enunciates

enunciating

enunciated

A: Good. You both did well.

A: Remember, the following terms are not valid English words:

pronunction

pronunciate

A: Most likely, if a speaker said proNOUNciation, the listener would understand.

A: If you said "pronounciate" it could be confusing for the listener.

A: This word has two problems, incorrect form and mispronunciation.

A: For example, "Can you pronounciate it?"

A: People can get confused by mispronounced terms.

Lesson 040

Describing Types of Oral Language

Teachers often find that introducing general categories works better after students have some experience. While it seems logical to start a lecture with a classification system, categories are often too abstract for students to use effectively. Therefore, giving students hands-on experience such as practicing pronunciation and struggling with mispronunciation is often better for easing students into a new area. After that, students can better understand the new topic because they have some practical experience to relate to the more conceptual description. In other words, deductive explanations are more easily comprehended after some inductive experience.

A: Listen to this audio clip.
A: Let me play that again. Where is the person from?
A: I wouldn't know unless I had checked.
A: Pronunciation or vocabulary, which is the best indicator? Listen again.
A: I had a hard time with the pronunciation, but the vocabulary was more difficult.
A: I will tell you now, Scotland. He is a native speaker of English from Scotland.
A: The point is that there are many ways to describe spoken language.
A: Several terms can be used to describe types of talking.
A: Some of the terms are speaking, conversation, pronunciation, and dialect.
A: I am going to select two readers.
A: Jean, seat 45, and Julie, seat 47.
A: Jean starts with the mic, and Julie uses the computer.
A: My lesson plan has four words for you to define and use in sentences.
A: Jean, please start, and switch with Julie after every line of text.
B: Speaking is talking aloud, which includes all forms of spoken language, conveying

information, and expressing thoughts and feelings.

C: Conservation is an informal spoken exchange in which two or more people speak together, exchange thoughts and feelings, or request information and answer questions.

B: Pronunciation means a way of speaking, or a distinct style of speech.

C: A dialect is a particular form of a language, including unique pronunciation, grammar, and vocabulary, of a group of people.

A: Jean and Julie, thanks, you may sit down.

A: We have just finished reading the definitions of four terms.

A: I want you to show me that you understand these vocabulary words.

A: Let's start with Heather, seat 23, and Freddy, seat 24.

A: Please come to the front.

A: Heather, you start. Please get the microphone.

A: Let's talk about the word "dialect," which means the way a group of people speak a language.

A: Heather, which accent is correct, British vs. American English?

A: Do you need a minute to prepare an answer?

B: Yes. We're not ready.

A: While you two prepare your answer, I am going to work the room for a few minutes.

A: I'm back. Heather, what is your answer?

D: Both are OK.

A: Good answer. OK. Now, please give me a longer and more complete answer.

D: American English is a dialect of British English.

A: Hmm... You introduced a new idea. I would say that American and British English are two different dialects.

A: However, your second answer did not address the question.

A: This is one possible answer, from my lesson plan.

A: No standard exists which can be used as a measure of right or wrong pronunciation.

A: Neither British nor American English is correct.

A: Freddy, you get this question.

A: Given the large number of people who speak English, what is the central issue regarding pronunciation?

E: Speaking correctly, it is hard.

A: That is a good answer, but not the point I was trying to make.

A: You have both answered a question, so you can sit down.

A: Good answers, and good microphone handling skill.

A: The question implicitly asks what is the goal of pronunciation activities in English class (or elsewhere), not what sounds are hard to make.

A: The answer is that the goal is clear communication.

A: The central issue means the main goal, and in this case it means pronunciation.

A: Whether in a language class or in conversation with people who speak the language, the main goal is to use the pronunciation necessary to help the listener understand what you are trying to say.

Lesson 041

Requiring Complete Sentences

Many students write only short answers using simple words. While they may answer the question correctly, minimal-phrase sentences rarely help student writers improve their language production. Forming complete thoughts is especially important for student writers in lower-level classes. The best term to describe well-developed thoughts is calling them complete sentences.

Teachers have to be able to identify incomplete sentences when they see student work displayed on the screen. Students know they should capitalize the first letter of the first word in the sentence, and they almost always get the terminal punctuation correct. However, the sentence structure between the capital letter and the final punctuation mark frequently needs rewriting. Given sentences with multiple errors, teachers have to prioritize the errors, and keep the rewriting process short. In order to avoid losing the attention of class members, the teacher must help the student writers while at the same time make a general writing point for the rest of the class.

After checking the point being practiced, teachers should examine student sentences from a structure point of view. Teachers can look at either the parts or the whole. The parts usually include spelling, grammar, and punctuation. In terms of the whole, teachers can check sentences, paragraphs, or the complete composition. Students still have trouble with simple, compound, and complex sentences. In any event, as a way to prioritize, teacher assessment of written work needs to be coordinated with the textbook but also with the major emphasis of the current lesson.

A: Our two student writers are hard at work at the classroom computer, and you can see their work on the screen as it develops.

A: They are writing a transitional sentence for the end of paragraph two and a topic sentence for the beginning of paragraph three.

A: You should be working on the same job.

A: If you finish that job, write the transitional sentence at the end of paragraph three and the topic sentence for paragraph four.

A: This text can be used for the composition which is due next week, so the more you do now the less you have to do at home.

A: I am going to start checking papers while we wait for our student writers.

A: I am going to check papers in this row.

A: Lisa, seat 33, you are first.

A: Lulu, seat 43, you are next.

A: Lisa, please underline the part of this transitional sentence which concludes paragraph two.

A: Good. Now underline the part of the sentence which introduces paragraph three.

A: OK. What is this phrase?

B: It's a connector.

A: I am glad to see that you are using the connectors on page 57, but there is a problem.

A: The first part, here, is a simple sentence.

A: The rain, subject, was coming down, verb, in buckets, object.

A: This is a simple sentence with a SVO structure.

A: The last section is also a simple sentence.

A: The people at the bus stop, subject, were, verb, dry, adjective.

A: Unfortunately, the connector contains a grammar problem.

A: Let me read it out loud.

A: "The rain was coming down in buckets, however, the people at the bus stop were dry."

A: How are the two simple sentences connected?

B: By this "however"?

A: Right. The ideas are connected, but what about the sentence structure?

A: How many sentences are in this line of text?

B: One?

A: It looks like two sentences.

A: Assuming it is two sentences, which sentence should the connector go with?

A: The second?

A: Correct.

A: What happens if you remove the connector and keep one comma?

A: It's a grammar problem.

A: Right. Good. Please fix it.

A: Lulu, before I check your paper, I need to ask the student writers if they are ready.

C: No hurry. Take your time.

A: Lulu, Lulu... That's funny. I'll be back.

Lesson 042

Correcting Sentence Structure Errors

Many students have trouble with sentence structure. Two of the main problems are comma splices and sentence fragments. Teachers who ask students to use the classroom computer to display their work need to edit the sentence while changing as little as possible of the student phrasing and content.

One common student writing problem is comma splices. A comma splice is usually two simple sentences combined with a comma, or it could be a simple sentence and a sentence fragment. Straightening out comma splices is difficult because many students are not clear about the relationships between independent and dependent clauses. Teachers need to show students how to check the S-V-O structure in the main clause. This can be done by drawing boxes around the S, V, and O parts of the main clause, and writing the appropriate letter over the respective box. Once the section of a sentence which contains the comma splice has been identified, students can correct the main clause. However, that usually means that part of the sentence is cut off. At this point, the student can decide what sort of additional information is necessary to make the sentence a fully-developed thought, and adding the severed part back into the sentence, or rewriting it to make it a separate sentence. After rechecking the content and the structure, the student writer needs to reconcile any remaining parts, but in practice this often results in deleting the leftover words or phrases.

Another common student writing problem is sentence fragments. Sentence fragments are grammatically incomplete lines of text. Many sentence fragments result from literally writing spoken language, and not converting spoken language to a more formal written language. The first step in fixing sentence fragments is drawing a box around the chunk of text. Since the fragment usually begins with a capital letter and ends with a period, students have trouble seeing it as a grammar problem. The next step is to look for the S-V-O parts of the line of text, which is the same process as resolving problems due to comma splices. Unlike comma splices, the main sentence is usually an incomplete sentence, so the student must determine what is missing. Simply adding a missing verb or object rarely solves the problem. Most of the time, other words need to be added, and the thought group needs to be checked to determine its meaning. The process of adjusting by adding words, changing the part of speech of a word, or deleting additional words takes a couple of iterations.

As an instructional technique, editing student sentences is a multifaceted process. It has to focus on the general course content while imparting knowledge about writing that touches on many points not included in the class. Since there are many ways to phrase an idea, the teacher has to look at what the student wrote, touch it up a little, and keep going without losing the momentum in the class. Many teachers feel nervous opening themselves up to this type of exercise, as they worry about not being able to fix the sentence or that they will display a lack of skill in front of students. Being a little nervous about this type of exercise is common enough, and not always having the right answer is always a possibility, but most teachers are much better writers than their students. The main impediment is most likely simple nervousness about doing something new. After practicing the technique a few times, most teachers will start to feel more comfortable, and they will be able to handle any sentence on the screen.

A: Molly, seat 48, and Helen, seat 49, have finished their sentences.

A: Please stop writing, and let's take a look.

A: Everybody has been writing sentences with gerunds as objects of prepositions.

A: Molly, did you write the first sentence?

B: Yes.

A: OK. Molly, you have to enter the changes since you wrote the sentence.

A: Helen, when we suggest changes for your sentence, you get the keyboard.

A: Let me read the first sentence for a minute.

A: Everybody in the class should do the same thing.

A: Look at the top sentence, and think about the gerund and the sentence structure.

A: Molly, select your sentence, but you don't have to highlight with a background color.

A: I just want everybody to be clear which sentence we are looking at.

A: I can see that there is a problem with the usage of the phrase the textbook is teaching on page 78, and I can see a second error.

A: The second error is a comma splice, but it might also be called a sentence fragment depending on how you look at it.

A: We don't have a lot of time, so we will only discuss these two errors.

A: Molly, the grammar topic is gerunds as an object of a preposition, and you are missing a preposition.

A: Everybody, check the grammar box on page 78, and think about where to put the missing preposition.

A: Molly, add the preposition "of" after the word "tired."

A: What should the phrase be?

B: Uh… "tired of working"?

A: Correct. Good job.

A: Now, your sentence includes a comma, and it is followed by "thanks for asking," which is a common spoken language phrase but in this class, with its emphasis on formal English writing, it is a sentence fragment.

A: For now, change the comma to a period, and capitalize the T of thanks.

A: This is still an informal spoken language phrase, but we will take it for now.

A: Good job, Molly.

A: Helen, your turn.

A: Grab the mouse and select your sentence.

A: Everybody, read the highlighted sentence, and start the process again.

Lesson 043

Explaining Evaluation

Teachers should explain the purpose of evaluation to students. They should explain that the primary goal of evaluation is checking if the students have learned the skills. Student evaluation means scoring and assessment by the teacher during the course. Students receive scores and comments on individual assignments. To analyze writers' compositions, teachers should use a grading key to make sure that the parts being checked represent the topics being emphasized. With sufficient error correction in class, teachers can reduce error correction on homework. One method for providing student feedback in class is to walk around the classroom, checking students' papers, giving suggestions, and focusing students' attention on the aspects of the essay, which are being taught and evaluated. Another method for providing student feedback on their writing is to assign student writers the job of composing on the computer, and then commenting on the displayed text. While the class members watch, student writers receive feedback from the teacher, and they enter the specified revisions. This type of feedback helps the students working individually in their seats as well as the student writers working on the classroom computer.

Grades are one of the few parts of school which motivate students. Teachers need to use a grading system to evaluate students, communicate information, and direct effort to particular aspects of curriculum and instruction. A robust grading system allows evaluation to be used as a part of the instructional system, which means that it has value beyond the simple purpose of reporting the score on an assignment. Grading systems take a lot of time, but they are one of the central elements of instruction. The grading system needs to be designed and developed before the class, implemented from the first day, and simplified for students to understand. By coordinating curriculum, instruction, and evaluation, teachers can increase the effectiveness of their classes. This type of grading system will increase the ability of students to benefit from teacher evaluation.

An important part of any grading system is the grade range. An effective grade range is 70 to 90. Some students rise above it, and other students sink below it. Most teachers are unable to promise to keep students within the passing zone between 100 and 60, but they can scale graded items in such a way as to set up a range that traverses the zone. When a criteria-based grading system starts at 100, points are subtracted. For example, if teachers give a quiz with ten items, they can make each item four points, which means that the effective grade range starts at 100 and goes down to 60. Even if students are unable to answer every question, they still end up with a passing grade, which is 60. When teachers give students failing grades, it is a very strong message about students' performance. Any grade below 60 is failing, but the lower the number, the more it hurts the students' average. To avoid decimating students' averages, and making the hole too deep for them to climb out, teachers should give them the highest possible failing grades. Teachers should give students a 59 when they fail in order to send a message they are failing while preventing them from having an average so low they are unable to pass the class. Throw in a couple of tough questions, and nobody will get a 100, which brings the top score down to 88 or 92. Grades are the only leverage teachers have, so it is important to use them to motivate rather than punish.

A: Evaluation takes many forms.

A: Most of the work you do in the class will not be evaluated.

A: When I say evaluated, I mean reviewed using grading criteria and placing a score on the bottom of the paper.

A: There is too much English being generated for the teacher to check every word and grade every utterance and line of text.

A: For most of the class, students have to follow the language being produced and check the corrections and suggestions for improvement in order to apply the insights to their work.

A: Every class I walk around the classroom and make suggestions, which is a form of evaluation, but there is no grade attached to this process.

A: Every student will be selected as a reader or writer, and then the language produced will be subjected to a thorough review.

A: At such times, the evaluation of the work will be public and focused on a small sample.

A: For student readers and writers, no grade is given though they do get a contribution point for going to the front and doing a job.

A: Of course, this class has numerous graded in-class and homework activities.

A: These items are graded, and scores are produced.

A: Student scores will be displayed regularly, which helps people evaluate progress.

A: When I grade work, I use a grading key, which means I only check the items on the key.

A: This is a sampling technique, and I am checking a variety of things.

A: I check submission procedures, formatting, computer skills, writing, and speaking.

A: Once again, I am unable to check every word, so I sample the things that I am teaching you, and then you get a score based the sampled work.

A: It is impossible to add up the points on the grading key and determine how you got your grade.

A: I have a secret formula, where some factors are weighted more heavily, and some values are derived by multiplying by a weighting.

A: I can't tell you my secret come because it's ... a secret.

A: This multifactor system is fair and efficient.

A: Your job is to learn the skills being taught.

A: Don't worry because I can see your work, and I will give you credit for your hard work.

A: Grading can help student by focusing their attention, and it can provide feedback on their ability to complete tasks which represent the English being taught.

A: However, that is just an overt part of schooling, and does not represent inner learning autonomy.

A: In the end, student graduate and start working, and at that time they have to keep teaching themselves.

A: They must develop the ability to evaluate their own work and improve it.

A: In a sense, they have to develop their own grading criteria, and measure their own performance based on their own criteria.

A: Of course, external sources of control will exert an influence on their work, but the best system for meeting these requirements is internal.

See Appendix 43.1 for Grading Key Example.

Lesson 044

Displaying Grades and Line Graphs

Grade systems and grade distributions can be displayed during class. If students understand their performance, and their current status in a course, they have greater comfort in the class and control over their participation. Withholding or obscuring grade data hurts the teacher because some students will become nervous, uncooperative, and argumentative. Since many universities prohibit teachers from displaying student data that openly identifies individuals, teachers should use a system to anonymize the data, and then they can project it with only the code to keep individual identities confidential.

Teachers should display comprehensive grade data three or four times a semester, usually after big assignments. At such times, teachers should let students see several views of grade data, including numerical grade data and line charts with markers. The estimated course grade, based on points possible up to that time, should be presented. The line charts with markers allow students to see the overall grade distribution, including high score, low score, and the range in between, which calms their nerves. It helps them to trust claims by the teacher about keeping them in the grade range if they do the work. Furthermore, they can see how they compare with their peers. Moreover, students can check their individual grades and keep track of their current course grade based on points possible. In addition to displaying grades, teachers should present participation grade data. The participation grade is created from four measures, including class contribution, late to class, no textbook, and no quiz paper.

Given all this data entry, many teachers make mistakes, and displaying the full range of data makes it possible for students to check the accuracy of the teacher's spreadsheets. After being informed of an error, the teacher can correct it right away.

A: Get out the compositions which I returned.

A: If you didn't pick up your paper, it is here at the front.

A: This summary of student grades will start with your last homework and timed writing assignment.

A: It also includes the composition and timed writing I just returned.

A: This line chart shows the grade distribution for the composition.

A: Excluding the four students who did not hand in a paper, the grade range goes from 73 to 93.

A: Let me show you a couple more line charts, and then we will look at individual grades.

A: This line chart shows the scores from the recent textbook exercises.

A: You can see that six people did not hand in any work, and the range of those who did goes from 60 to 95.

A: Now, let's look at individual grades.

A: It's hard to see all the data at one time, especially from the back row.

A: You can see here that 65 percent of points possible have been determined.

A: If grades closed today, this would be your final grade, but we still have 35 percent to go.

A: Look at your grades.

A: I used your secret code, so as to present this grade data anonymously.

A: I am going to scroll down and show you the grading of the individual assignments.

A: Most of these numbers are on the grade key stapled to the front of your homework.

A: You can tell a lot about your skills from these grades.

A: Here are grammar points, and this section shows sentence structure.

A: If you have a high grammar sub-score, your grammar is good.

A: I don't review and score every word in every sentence.

A: It is impossible to process all those papers.

A: Last year, I read student essays containing about 660,000 words.

A: The average essay was about 350 words, and with from 22 essays from about 100 students over the whole year, it worked out this way.

A: Let me see... 30 times 22 times 100 equals 660,000.

A: Yikes, that was a lot of essays.

A: Instead, I use a sampling system, and you can see that I sample a variety of areas with which I have been helping you.

A: For example, this sub-score reflects your formatting and word processing skill.

A: Moving right along, the next four line charts show the participation measures.

A: We don't have a problem with students arriving late in the class.

A: Based on this table, you can see that several students have a problem arriving on time, but the vast majority of students in this class arrive on time. Good job.

A: Likewise, this table shows you that you are doing well bringing your textbook to class. Good job.

A: If you see any grades which I entered wrong, please tell me.

A: I enter a lot of data, and I make mistakes.

A: I am always happy to talk to students about grades.

A: See me before class, during the break or after class, or you can come to my office.

A: Now, it is time to get out your textbooks.

See Appendix 44.1 for Grade Spreadsheet.
See Appendix 44.2 Line Graph with Markers.

Lesson 045

Trying New Instructional Activities

Many university-level lecture classes feature a teacher on a platform at the front, projecting PPT slides and explaining the concepts. It was hoped that students can comprehend the material and absorb the information. However, a look at the rest of the classroom tells a different story. Students eat and drink, chat and check their phones, arrive late and drift in and out of the lecture, and many feel no hesitation to put their heads down and go to sleep. The teacher might interrupt the lecture to comment on student behavior from time to time, but many continue with the same instructional system after making comments about "paying attention." The problem with telling students to "stop messing around" is that many of them think that off-task activities are often more interesting than lectures. However, disconnected students can be drawn back into class activities by something that they regard more valuable than playing with their phones.

The Hands-On English Teaching system described in this book is based on teachers coaching students during increasingly difficult practice activities. The system gives students more involvement, by offering students the opportunity to exhibit their ability of speaking and writing. By the process of individualization, teachers spend more time individually helping the students. The underlying motivation for personal improvement in turn overrides the feeling of boredom in class. Combining heightened personal motivation and increased desire to improve their language skills is the basis for Hands-On English Teaching.

This system has many advantages, especially the major benefit of increasing student involvement. The students who work as computer operators, readers and writers are definitely more involved as they participate in the upfront part of the activities. The rest of the students in the seats are more involved as the teachers works the room and they observe their classmates. The best way for teachers to see that this proposition is true involves trying it in class, and watching the increased student involvement. This instructional system involves many parts and simultaneous processes, and teachers need to practice in order to coordinate the elements of the system.

To begin, teachers can practice the parts individually before using the whole system. Teachers who adopt parts will realize gains, but using the whole system will produce greater benefits than selective incorporation of individual parts. Whether adopted in part or as a whole, teachers will immediately see increased participation and student learning. The key is that the teacher coaches the students while they practice speaking and writing activities. If students are assigned jobs such as reader, writer, and computer operator, and the teacher guides them through increasingly difficult English speaking and writing activities, students will be on task. That is the process that needs to be added to applied English classes.

This is just one of the many ways that teachers help students. Some instructional systems are simple, and others are complicated. Older teaching methods, namely lectures and exams, are in the process of being reformed. This new instructional system is part of the reform effort. The main point is not that the new system is an option for teachers, but that all the teaching and learning activities in this system increase time on task. Time on task and student participation make Hands-On English teaching a system worth trying.

A: Today, I am going to try something new.

A: I am going to ask for two students to come to the front and read part of my lesson plan.

A: After that, I am going to ask two students to use the net on the classroom computer, and copy the definitions of the selected vocabulary words for you.

A: If that isn't enough, I am going to ask two more students to write sentences which incorporate the vocabulary words.

A: You might be wondering where I will be if the students are up at the front of the room, and I'm not "teaching" the class.

A: No, I won't be going to Starbucks.

A: I will be walking up and down the aisles of the classroom, checking papers and helping students.

A: How does that sound?

A: If that sounds OK to you, then we will get right to it.

A: We will start with a guy who can't be stopped when he gets going.

A: Tank, seat 56, get up here.

A: Tank, who do you want to help you? Who should I pick to help you?

B: Maybe… August.

A: OK, August, seat 33, your presence is being requested.

A: August, help us out. Get on up here.

A: It's time to try a new instructional technique.

C: I'm ready. Let's do it.

Index

Assessing student work, 135
Assigned seats, 25
Assigned seats, Appendix 3.1, 148
Attendance, 33
Biobooks, 60
Biopage 01 Handout, Appendix 16.1, 152
Biopage 02 Handout, Appendix 16.2, 154
Biopages, 64, 66
Breaks, 35
Cell phones, 47
Chalk, Walk, and Talk, 11-13
Class coverage tool, 117, 174
Class rules, 38
Class Rules, Appendix 8.1, 149
Class time, 31
Classroom contribution, 94
Classroom data, 85
Classroom computer, 15, 86, 109
Coaching students, 101, 105, 109
Comma splices, 129, 132
Complete sentences, 129
Computer operator, 109
Contribution, 94
Contribution Checklist, Appendix 31.1, 167
Conversation activities, 126
Displaying grades, 139
Displaying lesson plans, 50
Displaying line charts, 139
Distractions, 47
Document filenames, 71, 81, 161
Drinks, 47
Editing student sentences, 132
Entering data, 85
Evaluation, 135
Filename Structure, Appendix 22.1, 161
Food, 47
Four-skill course, 20
Grades, 135, 139
Grading keys, 159, 175
Grade distributions, 139, 177
Greeting students, 42
Guiding students, 101, 105, 109
Header Format Instructions, Appendix 19.2, 69-70, 157
Header paper, 69-70
Header Paper Sample, Appendix 19.1, 157
Homework, uploading, 75, 77, 79, 81, 161
Informal writing errors, 105-108, 175
Instructional activities, 142
Introduction, 7-16
Late Arrivals, Appendix 27.1, 44, 150
Late Student Sign-in Sheet, Appendix 10.1, 150
Lesson Plan Sample, Appendix 35.1, 168

Lesson plans, 50, 112
Mispronunciation, 120, 123
Names, English, Chinese, Pinyin, 29, 60, 64
No food, drinks, phones, 47
Online submission, 75
Online Submission, Appendix, 22.1, 161
Paper copies, 60, 71, 83
Paper security, 77
PowerPoint, 50, 55, 112
Projection, 35, 112
Pronunciation, 120, 123
Readers, 101
Scoring papers, 135
Secret codes, 73
Secret Codes, Appendix 21.1, 160
Sentence fragments, 117, 132
Sentence structure errors, 132
Starting time, 22
Student computer operators, 11-16, 94, 109, 142
Student data, collecting, 85, 88
Student data spreadsheets, 90
Student feedback, 135
Student presenters, 11-16, 25, 98
Student readers, 24, 58, 94, 101
Student writers, 11-16, 54, 93, 105, 129
Submission, papers, 75, 81, 161
Taking attendance, 33
Teacher computer, 10, 15, 86, 109
Teacher notes, 88
Textbooks, checking, 55
Textbook activities, 115
Textbooks, 24, 47, 52
Time on task, 11-16, 22, 31, 33, 85
Types of oral language, 126
Upload procedures, 75, 81, 161
Word stress, 120, 123

Appendix

3.1 Assigned Seats

Fall 2019 ENG250-24 (Tuesday) Seat Numbers

7/15/2019

1	余[][]	24	王[][]
2	劉[][]	25	盧[][]
3	呂[][]	26	莫[][]
4	周[][]	27	葉[][]
5	唐[][]	28	蔡[][]
6	宋[][]	29	蔡[][]
7	康[][]	30	蔣[][]
8	張[][]	31	蕭[][]
9	張[][]	32	蕭[][]
10	張[][]	33	薛[][]
11	張[][]	34	蘇[][]
12	張[][]	35	許[][]
13	張[][]	36	謝[][]
14	李[][]	37	賴[][]
15	李[][]	38	邱[][]
16	李[][]	39	邱[][]
17	林[][]	40	鄭[][]
18	林[][]	41	陳[][]
19	林[][]	42	高[][]
20	林[][]	43	高[][]
21	楊[][]	44	黃[][]
22	江[][]	45	黃[][]
23	熊[][]	46	黃[][]

8.1 Class Rules

Food, Drink, Phones, and Sleeping

You can't learn when you are playing with a small god in your sleep.
你睡著就只能找周公學習了。
Ni shuizhao jiu zhineng zhao zhougong xuexi le.

If you are reading a text message and the textbook at the same time, you can't concentrate.
上課看簡訊又看書會讓你無法專心。
Shangke kanjianxun you kanshu hui rang ni wufazhuanxin.

You can't speak in class when you have food in your mouth.
上課吃東西就無法與老師暢所欲言了。
Shangke chidongxi jiu wufa yu laoshi changsuoyuyan le.

You can't deal with notes when your left hand holds a phone and right hand holds a teacup.
當你左手握電話，右手拿茶杯時，就沒手應付筆記了。
Dang ni zuoshuo wo dianhua, youshuo na chabei shi, jiu meishou yingfu biji le.

Alex's Attendance Policy

Seats are assigned using the order number from the class roster.
座位以點名表上的序號為準。
Zuowei yi dianmingbiao shang de shuhao weizhun.

I take attendance by checking to see if you are sitting in your assigned seat.
每堂課我會依座位表點名。
Meitang ke wo hui yi zuowei dianming.

I upload attendance after every class.
每一堂課我會上網登入你的出缺勤紀錄。
Meiyitang ke wo hui shangwang dengru ni de chuqueqin jilu.

If you are more than 10 minutes late, sign in on the paper at the front by writing time, Chinese and English name, student ID, and assigned seat number.
如果遲到 10 分鐘，要來到老師座位前登記你的中、英文名字，學號，還有點名表上的序號。
Ruguo chidao shi fengzhong, yaolaidao laoshi zuowei qian dengji ni de zhong ying wen mingzi xuehao haiyou dianmingbiao shang de xuhao.

Late at the start of class more than 15 minutes then absent for first period.
上課遲到超過 15 分鐘算第一堂課曠課。
Shangke chidao chaoguo shiwu fenzhong suan diyitangke kuangke.

10.1 Late Student Sign-in Sheet

Fall 2019 Late Student Sign-In Sheet
10/7/2019

If you are more than 5 minutes late, fill in arrival time, seat number, student ID, Chinese name, English name, and reason.

如果遲到 5 分鐘，要登記你的抵達的時間、座位號碼、學號、還有中、英文名字。

Arrival Time	Seat Number	Student ID	Chinese Name	English Name	Reason

12.1 Course Schedule LANG107 Spring 2019

Monday	Lesson	Unit	Due
02/18	L1	U07	Classes Begin
02/25	L2	U07	Bio-01
03/04	L3	U07	
03/11	L4	U07	U7 Composition-Oral
03/18	L5	U08	Bio-02
03/25	L6	U08	
04/01			Spring Break
04/08	L7	U08	U8 Composition-Oral
04/15			Mid-Term Exam
04/22	L8	U09	Word-Cloud-01
04/29	L9	U09	
05/06	L10	U09	
05/13	L11		U9 Composition-Oral
05/20	L12	U10	
05/27	L13	U10	
06/03	L14	U10	
06/10	L15		U10 Composition-Oral
06/17			Final Exam

16.1 Biopage 01 Handout

ENG250, Fall 2019, Bio 01
10/7/2019

Follow the format in the example.
照著例子上面的格式。
Zhaozhe lizi shangmian de geshi.

Use computer to do all homework.
用電腦做所有的功課。
Yong diannao zuosuoyou de gongke.

Print one copy of every homework assignment.
每份作業都要列印一份。
Meifen zuoye douyao lieyin yifen.

Please submit homework on time.
請按時交作業。
Qing anshi jiao zuoye.

Upload another copy to Dropbox.
上傳備份到 Dropbox。
Shangchuan beifen dao Dropbox.

I accept late homework for two weeks.
我會收遲交兩個禮拜以內的作業。
Wo hui shou chijiao liangge libai yinei de zuoye.

If homework is late, then your grade will be half.
如果作業遲交，你的分數就會折半。
Ruguo zuoye chijiao, ni de fenshu jiuhui zheban.

After two weeks, late homework will not be accepted and the grade will be 0.
我不會收超過兩個禮拜交的作業，且成績以零分計算。
Wo buhui shou chaoguo liangge libai jiao de zuoye, qie chenji yi lingfen jisuan.

Bio 01

AR Notes

Name (English)	Alex Rath
Name (Chinese)	徐國華
Name (Pinyin)	Hsu Guo-hua
Student ID Number	A105320021
Seat Number	01
Class and Section	ENG250-01
Class Day and Time	Monday 10:10-12:00

16.2 Biopage 02 Handout

ENG250, Fall 2019, Bio 02
10/7/2019

Follow the format in the example.
照著例子上面的格式。
Zhaozhe lizi shangmian de geshi.

Use computer to do all homework.
用電腦做所有的功課。
Yong diannao zuosuoyou de gongke.

Print one copy of every homework assignment.
每份作業都要列印一份。
Meifen zuoye douyao lieyin yifen.

Please submit homework on time.
請按時交作業。
Qing anshi jiao zuoye.

Upload another copy to Dropbox.
上傳備份到 Dropbox。
Shangchuan beifen dao Dropbox.

I accept late homework for two weeks.
我會收遲交兩個禮拜以內的作業。
Wo hui shou chijiao liangge libai yinei de zuoye.

If homework is late, then your grade will be half.
如果作業遲交，你的分數就會折半。
Ruguo zuoye chijiao, ni de fenshu jiuhui zheban.

After two weeks, late homework will not be accepted and the grade will be 0.
我不會收超過兩個禮拜交的作業，且成績以零分計算。
Wo buhui shou chaoguo liangge libai jiao de zuoye, qie chenji yi lingfen jisuan.

Bio 02

AR Notes

Name (English)	Alex Rath
Name (Chinese)	徐國華
Name (Pinyin)	Hsu Guo-hua
Student ID Number	A105320021
Seat Number	01
Class and Section	ENG-318-01
Class Day and Time	Monday 10:10-12:00

Hometown	Wenshan District, Taipei, Taiwan
Junior High School	Wanfang Junior High School
Senior High School	Wanfang Senior High School
Major at SHU	English
Double Major	No
Minor	No
Transfer Student	Yes
Previous College	China University of Technology
Major at Previous College	Computer Science

19.1 Header Paper Sample

Name (English)	Alex Rath
Name (Chinese)	徐國華
Name (Pinyin)	Hsu Guo-hua
Student ID Number	A107320021
Seat Number	12
Class and Section	LANG107-12
Class Day and Time	Monday 3:10

19.2 Header Format Instructions

ENG250 Fall 2019 Header Format Instructions
2019/10/7

For each assignment, students should submit one paper copy in class and upload one digital copy to appropriate ENG250 Dropbox account.

Header

All work submitted by students should contain the Header at the top of the first page.

	Name (English)	Alex Rath
	Name (Chinese)	徐國華
	Name (Pinyin)	Hsu Guo-hua
	Student ID Number	A107320001
	Seat Number	01
	Class and Section	ENG250-01
	Class Day and Time	Wednesday 10:10-12:00

20.1 Composition-01

	Name (English)	Alex Rath
	Name (Chinese)	徐國華
	Name (Pinyin)	Hsu Guo-hua
	Student ID Number	A105320021
	Seat Number	12
	Class and Section	ENG318-02
	Class Day and Time	Monday 8:00

The Benefits of Government-Funded Infrastructure

Many people complain about one part of society, as it seems to control everything in their lives. While it is true that government dictates a seemingly endless list of laws and regulations, modern society could not function without it. All the while, they complain about taxes, but they overlook the way that tax dollars are spent on the public good, such as storm drains, which prevent flooding, and street lights, which make driving at night safe. From stop signs to airports, infrastructure, the basic physical and organizational structures such as buildings, roads, power plants needed for the operation of cities and town, is essential to modern life. One of the most important contributions of government is developing and maintaining infrastructure.

Citizens complain endlessly about taxes and infrastructure. Drivers love to complain about construction of roads and the time lost due to traffic delays. They say driving is slower than walking. When two lanes narrow to one, and slowly moving cars pass by a seemingly idle construction worker, many people make comments about tax dollar at work helping the guy get a tan and paying him to check his messages. These reckless drivers and selfish whiners forget that the system was designed for all members of society, not just vehicle owners, and blame government as if it was the problem, not a solution.

Developing and maintaining infrastructure is one of the most important contributions of government. Designing, developing, and maintaining infrastructure is a direct application of public money collected through taxation for the public good. Despite the amount of infrastructure all around the cities and towns where people live, they rarely see it as government dollars at work. In fact, they take it for granted, and some people take if for personal usage. From big corporations which run fleets of delivery trucks to the homeowners who park on the sidewalk in front of their residences, everybody uses the infrastructure provided by government and fails to even see it. Without out this infrastructure, people could hardly go anywhere. Due to the infrastructure built and managed the government, people can enjoy in a better quality of life.

Words: 389

Composition 1-2

ENG250 Fall 2019 Grading Key	
Paper (in Class)	
Digital (Online)	
Locked + Encrypted	
Header Format	
Body Format	
Three Paragraphs	
Formal Writing Style	
Cause and Effect	
Public Transportation	
Character Border	
P1 Thesis, P3 Restated Thesis.	
Character Shading	
P1 Hook, P3 SOP	
Underlining Function	
P2 Comparative Form	

21.1 Secret Codes

ENG250 Secret Code Form
10/7/2019

In order to present grade and participation data in class, all students need to submit a secret code. The secret code will be used in place of student names and ID numbers when personal data is projected in class. In addition, use the secret code when encrypting and locking work to be uploaded for the class.

Complete the Name and ID Box.

Name (English)	
Name (Chinese)	
Name (Pinyin)	
Student ID Number	
Seat Number	
Class and Section	
Class Day and Time	

Secret Code Form

Write a secret code which is 4-7 English letters and numbers in length for use in this class.

22.1 Online Submission

ENG250 Fall 2019 Homework Procedures
2019/10/7

All homework needs to be uploaded to the class Dropbox account. Use this process to upload locked and encrypted homework.

Upload

Upload one locked and encrypted digital copy of each assignment to Dropbox (www.dropbox.com) before the date and time when the assignment is due in class.

Dropbox account: rattle@mail.shu.edu.tw

Dropbox password: submit

Put the assignment work in the correct folder:

ENG250-01 (Wednesday 3-4)
ENG250-02 (Tuesday 1-2)
ENG250-03 (Wednesday 1-2)
ENG250-04 (Monday1-2)
ENG250-05 (Thursday 1-2)

When uploading documents to Dropbox, use the ENG250 system for filenames.
If, for example, a student is in ENG250 Section 1, use this filename:

ENG250-01-Seat01-A107320001-Bio01-20190901.docx

ENG250	01	Seat01	A107320001	Bio01	20190901	docx
Course	Section	Seat No.	SHU ID No.	Assignment	Date	File Type

ENG250 Fall 2018 Header, Upload, and Encrypt
2019/10/7

Encrypt

To lock and encrypt a MS Word document (= .doc or .docx file), go to the File menu.

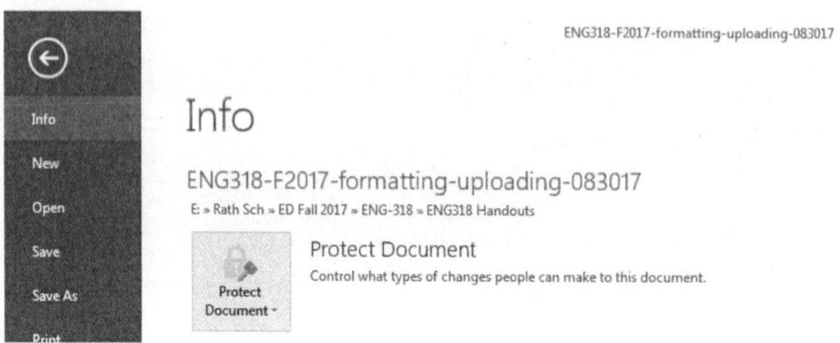

Select Protect Document.

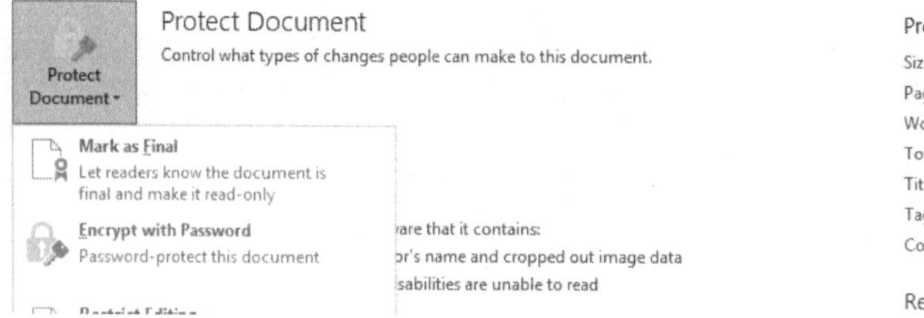

Use the ENG250 secret code to encrypt each file uploaded to Dropbox.

26.1 Audio-01 Assignment

Name (English)	Alex Rath
Name (Chinese)	徐國華
Name (Pinyin)	Hsu Guo-hua
Student ID Number	A107320001
Seat Number	01
Class and Section	ENG250-03
Class Day and Time	Wednesday 8:10-10:00

Audio-01 Description
This assignment focuses on the identification of multisyllabic words that receive special word stress and the recording of a text that allows students to practice their English speaking skills including the words which receive special word stress.

Requirements
Find an article in the *New York Times*. Create a one-page paper which includes the online address of the student's oral recording, the title of the NYT article, 200-250 words from the article, and online address of the article. Place on required class header paper, put the title of the assignment under the header on the left, and follow that with these items in the following order:

Online address of the student's oral recording
The title of the NYT article
About 200-250 words from the article
Online address of the article

Word Stress and IPA
The goal of this speaking activity is practice word stress, which can be reviewed in our textbook on pages A2, A3, and A5. For every multisyllabic word, check the word stress. If the word stress in on any syllable other than the first, then place the IPA pronunciation notation after the word. Other pronunciation notation which indicates word stress is welcome. This is an example:

> SPERRYVILLE, Va. — "The Sanford Guide to Antimicrobial /ˌan-ti-mī-ˈkrō-bē-əl/ Therapy" is a medical handbook that recommends /rɛkəˈmɛnd/ the right amount /əˈmaʊnt/ of the right drug for treating ailments from bacterial /bakˈtɪərɪəl/ pneumonia /njuːˈməʊnɪə/ to infected /ɪnˈfɛktɪd/ wounds. Lives depend /dɪˈpɛnd/ on it.

See the full-page example on the reverse side of this handout.

Name (English)	Alex Rath
Name (Chinese)	徐國華
Name (Pinyin)	Hsu Guo-hua
Student ID Number	A107320001
Seat Number	01
Class and Section	ENG250-03
Class Day and Time	Wednesday 8:10-10:00

Audio-01
This is the website address of my Audio-01 recording:
--- insert youtube address here ---

What Happens After Amazon's Domination /dɒmɪˈneɪʃ(ə)n/ Is Complete /kəmˈpliːt/? Its Bookstore Offers Clues

SPERRYVILLE, Va. — "The Sanford Guide to Antimicrobial /ˌan-ti-mī-ˈkrō-bē-əl/ Therapy" is a medical handbook that recommends /rɛkəˈmɛnd/ the right amount /əˈmaʊnt/ of the right drug for treating ailments from bacterial /bakˈtɪərɪəl/ pneumonia /njuːˈməʊnɪə/ to infected /ɪnˈfɛktɪd/ wounds. Lives depend /dɪˈpɛnd/ on it.

It is not the sort of book a doctor should puzzle over, wondering, "Is that a '1' or a '7' in the recommended /ˌrɛkəˈmɛndɪd/ dosage?" But that is exactly /ɪɡˈzak(t)li/ the possibility /ˌpɒsɪˈbɪlɪti/ that has haunted the guide's publisher, Antimicrobial /ˌan-ti-mī-ˈkrō-bē-əl/ Therapy, for the past two years as it confronted /kənˈfrʌnt/ a flood of counterfeits — many of which were poorly printed and hard to read — in Amazon's vast bookstore.

"This threatens a bunch of patients — and our whole business," said Scott Kelly, the publisher's vice president.

Mr. Kelly's problems arise /əˈrʌɪz/ directly /dɪˈrɛktli / from Amazon's domination /dɒmɪˈneɪʃ(ə)n/ of the book business. The company sells substantially /səbˈstanʃ(ə)li/ more than half of the books in the United /juːˈnʌɪtɪd/ States, including /ɪnˈkluːdɪŋ/ new and used physical volumes as well as digital and audio formats. Amazon is also a platform for third-party sellers, a publisher, a printer, a self-publisher, a review /rɪˈvjuː/ hub, a textbook supplier /səˈplʌɪə/ and a distributor /dɪˈstrɪbjʊtə/ that now runs its own chain of brick-and-mortar stores.

But Amazon takes a hands-off approach /əˈprəʊtʃ/ to what goes on in its bookstore, never checking the authenticity /ɔːθɛnˈtɪsɪti/, much less the quality, of what it sells. It does not oversee /əʊvəˈsiː/ the sellers who have flocked to its site in any organized way.

https://www.nytimes.com/2019/06/23/technology/amazon-domination-bookstore-books.html?action=click&module=Top%20Stories&pgtype=Homepage

Audio 1-2 Grading Key

ENG250 Fall 2019 Grading Key	Audio 1-2
Paper (in Class)	
Digital (Online)	
Locked + Encrypted	
Header Format	
Body Format	
Assignment Name	
NYT Article	
Student Audio URL	
NYT Title	
NYT Article	
NYT URL	
Word Stress in Text	
Word Stress Notation	

27.1 Late Arrivals

Spring 2019 ENG318-03 (Thursday) Late to Class

5/16/2019

	Code	2/21	3/7	3/14	3/21	3/28	4/11	4/18	4/25	5/2	5/9	5/16	Total
1	J288118				-1	-1		-1					-3
2	Huang06												0
3	60401												0
4	S8NK666		-1				-1					-1	-3
5	n861228												0
6	m870520												0
7	jack087												0
8	YGO233												0
9	happy32		-1			-1			-1				-3
10	superm2												0
11	6987BBQ		-1										-1
12	MY1220		-1										-1
13	EQ048EQ										-1		-1
14	320095	-1	-1			-1					-1	-1	-5
15	870715		-1										-1
16	861113	-1	-1										-2
17	870604												0
18	F3RRAR1												0
19	0928												0
20	dyc1997	-1							-1	-1			-3
21	S2012	-1							-1	-1			-3
22	SHA28	-1										-1	-2
23	hua5840												0
		-5	-7	0	-1	-3	-1	-1	-3	-2	-2	-3	

31.1 Contribution Checklist

Spring 2019 ENG318-03 (Thursday) Contribution
5/30/2019

		Oral				Written			Comp	Total
	Code	Tot	O	O	O	W1	W2	W3	Net	
1	J288118	7				2				9
2	Huang06	7				2				9
3	60401	2				0				2
4	S8NK666	7				1				8
5	n861228	7				2				9
6	m870520	7				2				9
7	jack087	7				2				9
8	YGO233	8				2				10
9	happy32	6				2				8
10	superm2	7				2				9
11	6987BBQ	7				2				9
12	MY1220	6				3				9
13	EQ048EQ	6				3				9
14	320095	7				2				9
15	870715	7				2				9
16	861113	6				2				8
17	870604	7				2				9
18	F3RRAR1	7				2				9
19	0928	7				2				9
20	dyc1997	2				2				4
21	S2012	7				2				9
22	SHA28	3				1				4
23	hua5840	0				0				0

35.1 Lesson Plan Sample

ENG-318 Spring 2019 Lesson 13
5/01/2019

Take attendance.

Check schedule.

Missing Handouts

I still have some copies of the EU5 handout. Does anybody need one?

Today, we will look at part of Essay 19, and we will review Essays 20 and 21 in the following weeks.

I have decided to skip Unit 6. (Yeah!)

Modals

Review the section in the textbook entitled *Controlling Tone with Modals* on page 123.

Paragraph two identifies terms that strengthen or weaken verbs.

Stronger:
- Must
- Had better

Weaker:
- May
- Might
- Should
- Can
- Could

To assert (strengthen) a point use *must* and *had better*.

Use this when arguing your point.

Personally, I think *should* increases strength, but the authors categorize it as a modal that softens tone.

If it is in the middle, *should* is not as strong as *must*, but it is stronger than *can*.

To weaken (acknowledge but deride) an opponent's point use *may, might, could, can,* and *would.*

Here are two examples.

> John thinks the website <u>must</u> be entertaining as well as informative.
>
> John thinks the website <u>can</u> be entertaining as well as informative.

Although the meaning is a little different, *must* is stronger than *can.*

Now, read this sign, and think about how the modal changes the meaning.

Display pic.

If you went to the restroom in a restaurant, which sign would you rather see?

> *Employees must wash hands after using the bathroom.*
>
> *Employees might wash hands after using the bathroom.*

Select a student to explain both sentences.

Review student explanation.

Answer
↓
↓
↓
↓
↓
↓
The first sentence states a required action to employees.

The phrase *must wash hands* means they are required to use soap and water.

The second sentence describes the probability employees performed the required action.

The expression *might wash hands* means some employees wash their hands while others leave the bathroom without washing.

Here is better example:

Students must wear uniforms.
(required)
Students should wear uniforms.
(recommended)
Students can wear uniforms.
(optional)

By changing the modal verb, the meaning of the sentence changes.

Be careful about changing the meaning when using modal verbs.

Now you try it.

Write three sentences with varying modal verbs that address the same point.

Select two students.

Review student writing.

In this unit, the authors have combined instruction on modals and *if*-clauses because they work well together.

If-Clauses

Today, I want to focus on the past form of the *if*-clause.

Another name for this construction is the hypothetical conditional (also called unreal conditional).

Hypothetical means based on or serving as a hypothesis.

Conditional means subject to one or more conditions or requirements being met.

When used together, this phrase means that something might have happened, but it never occurred.

For example:

Jimmy might have brought coffee for everybody, but he was unable to carry 20 cups from 7-Eleven.

It would have been nice, but it never happened.

Now, I will convert this idea into an *if*-clause.

If Jimmy <u>had bought</u> cookies for everybody, the students <u>would have</u> gotten a snack.

Look at the verbs.

In the *if* statement, use the past perfect.

The past perfect tense is *had* + past participle.

The past participle of a regular verb is the base verb plus *-ed* or the past participle of an irregular verb.

My example of this tense is "had <u>bought</u>."

With an *if* statement, the past perfect usually

goes in the first half.

The modal verbs *could have*, *would have,* and *should have* are useful for expressing lost opportunities.

Past modals tell what *could have, would have,* and *should have* happened.

To form these past modals, use *could, would,* or *should* followed by *have*, and subsequently followed by a past participle verb.

For example:

Martha could have gone to any cafe she wanted to.

Matilda would have gone to the party, but she was tired.

Would have also forms the result clause of a past unreal conditional.

For example:

If I had known they were vegetarians, I would have brought a salad.

From https://learningenglish.voanews.com/a/grammar-would-have/3391128.html

Call these constructions unreal conditional or hypothetical conditional.

It reminds me of the phrase, "*I could have, I should have, I would have, but I didn't*," which is commonly evoked to signal regret.

Now, we turn our attention to writing.

Writing Practice

Write three *if-then* unreal conditional statements with past *if*-clause (see page 129) about school uniforms.

Select students.

Review student work.

Possible Answer
↓
↓
↓
↓
↓
↓
↓

If Stanley had worn his complete uniform, then the *jiàoguān* (教官) would not have stopped him at the front gate of the school.

I am sorry to say that Essay 19 (p. 116) does not contain a clear and useful example of an *if*-clause, but I will not argue the point with you.

Vocabulary

The word **argument** has several meanings.

Select a reader.

> The most common definition of argument is an exchange of diverging or opposite views, usually in an interaction which is a heated or angry exchange, and people who do so are often described as argumentative.

Display Pics 1-2.

Here is one last illustration of argument.

Examine Pic 03.

Who is correct?

Select students.

Answers
↓
↓
↓
↓
↓

↓

Answer 1: They both are correct.

Answer 2: Neither one is correct.

Answer 3: Alex! Stop messing with my mind. I want to actually learn something in this class.

Answer 4: The picture is an optical illusion.

More to the point, the word argument is commonly used to mean a reason, or set of reasons, given in support of an idea, action, or theory.

Argument essays are named in this way because they offer reasons to support an idea.

They are also called argumentative essays, persuasive essays, opinion essays, position papers, and think pieces.

Argument Essay Thesis Statement

Select readers.

-

A thesis statement for an argument essay needs a main idea and two reasons.

In an argument essay, a main idea has two parts.

-

The main idea includes an issue and a position on the issue.

The two reasons support the position.

-

In the thesis, no mention should be made of the counterargument or refutation.

Which one of these sentences is a thesis statement for an argument essay?

-

Select a new reader:

1 Entrance exams are big, crazy, and scary, and students feel the pressure of these exams.

2 Entrance exams should be eliminated because they fail to measure academic ability and produce too much stress.

-

Which one of these statements is a thesis statement for an argument essay?

Select a student.

Answer

↓

↓

↓

↓

↓

Sentence 2 is the thesis statement:

<u>Entrance exams should be eliminated because they fail to measure academic ability and produce too much stress.</u>

<u>Main idea (Issue and Position)</u>

<u>Issue: Entrance exams</u>

<u>Position: Should be eliminated</u>

<u>Two reasons</u>

<u>Reason 1: they fail to measure academic ability</u>

<u>Reason 2: they produce too much stress</u>

Argument Essay Structure

This is the structure of a five-paragraph argument essay.

When I say two reasons, it means the same thing as two arguments.

P1

Hook

Thesis Statement (Issue, position, and two reasons)

P2

Topic Sentence (Argument 1)

Transitional Sent

P3

Topic Sentence (Argument 2)

Transitional Sentence

P4

Counterargument

Refutation

Transitional Sentence

P5

Restated Thesis (Issue, position, and two reasons)

SOP

Textbook: Essay 19

Look at the thesis statement for Essay 19 (p. 116).

> *School uniforms are the better choice for three reasons.*
>
> Issue: *School uniforms*
> Position: *are the better choice*
> Reasons: *for three reasons.*

The authors use an indirect thesis (generally referring to the reasons), and in this class we always use a stated thesis (specifically mentioning the reasons).

Counterargument and Refutation

Review P5 (p. 116).

Select a reader.
Highlight the counterargument:

> Opponents of mandatory uniforms say that students who wear the same school uniforms cannot express their individuality.

Highlight the refutation:

> … school is a place to learn, not flaunt wealth and fashion.

Writing Practice

The topic is Student Essay 19 is as follows:

> Argue for or against school uniforms.

Write three sentences:

P1

Write a thesis statement (also called an argument):

> *School uniforms ---*

Remember, a thesis includes include an issue, position, and two reasons.

P4

Write a counterargument:

> *Opponents of* --- .

Remember, the counterargument addresses the position and the main reason in the argument.

P4

Write a refutation:

> *The opponents of <issue/position> are wrong because ---*

Remember, the refutation addresses the reason in the counterargument and reinforces the argument.

Write three sentences:
- Argument
- Counterargument

Refutation

If you finish these three sentences, work on the other structural sentences for SE19.

Next

Preview Essay 20, page 120.

37.1 Class Coverage Tool

Course and Section Day Date

Seat ____ Oral ☐ Written ☐	Seat ____ Oral ☐ Written ☐	Seat ____ Oral ☐ Written ☐	Seat ____ Oral ☐ Written ☐	Seat ____ Oral ☐ Written ☐	Seat ____ Oral ☐ Written ☐	Seat ____ Oral ☐ Written ☐	Seat ____ Oral ☐ Written ☐
Seat ____ Oral ☐ Written ☐	Seat ____ Oral ☐ Written ☐	Seat ____ Oral ☐ Written ☐	Seat ____ Oral ☐ Written ☐	Seat ____ Oral ☐ Written ☐	Seat ____ Oral ☐ Written ☐	Seat ____ Oral ☐ Written ☐	Seat ____ Oral ☐ Written ☐
Seat ____ Oral ☐ Written ☐	Seat ____ Oral ☐ Written ☐	Seat ____ Oral ☐ Written ☐	Seat ____ Oral ☐ Written ☐	Seat ____ Oral ☐ Written ☐	Seat ____ Oral ☐ Written ☐	Seat ____ Oral ☐ Written ☐	Seat ____ Oral ☐ Written ☐
Seat ____ Oral ☐ Written ☐	Seat ____ Oral ☐ Written ☐	Seat ____ Oral ☐ Written ☐	Seat ____ Oral ☐ Written ☐	Seat ____ Oral ☐ Written ☐	Seat ____ Oral ☐ Written ☐	Seat ____ Oral ☐ Written ☐	Seat ____ Oral ☐ Written ☐

43.1 Grading Key Example

LANG107 Spring 2019 U7 Composition-Oral Grading Key	
Paper (In Class)	
Digital (Online)	
Locked + Encrypted	
Header Format (Header, 2.5 CM Margins)	
U7 Composition	
Title Content and Format	
Text Format (Indentation, Double-spaced)	
Topic Sentence (Content/Grammar)	
Concluding Sentence (Content/Grammar)	
One Shaded Sentence	
Definition Sentence (Content/Grammar)	
Example (Content/Grammar)	
Informal Writing Errors	
U7 Oral	
Oral 3 Text Format	
Video 1 List (Term and IPA)	
Video 1 Oral Word Stress	
Video 1 Oral Sentence Stress	
Video 2 Text and Notation	
Video Oral Pauses	
Video Oral Micropauses	
Links to YouTube Video (Two)	

44.1 Grade Spreadsheet

Spring 2019 ENG318-03 (Thursday) Grades

5/19/2019

				5%	15%	3%	10%	3%	15%	3%	10%		65%	
			Code	Bio3	EU3	TB3	TWU3	Bio4	EU4	TB4	TWU4		Raw	Scaled
			n861228	95	91	100	92	100	92	100	91		60	92
			V9879	100	90	100	89	100	93	100	88		60	92
			870604	95	89	98	86	100	87	100	88		58	89
			m870520	95	79	94	92	100	92	100	87		58	89
			skyfish	85	77	100	91	100	90	100	92		57	88
			YGO233	85	86	94	89	100	86	88	84		56	87
			kiemi02	95	83	100	83	100	85	100	83		56	86
			S8NK666	85	87	94	81	100	90	90	78		56	86
			Huang06	90	83	100	70	100	86	100	83		55	84
			maroct	95	80	86	84	100	82	80	87		55	84
			taurus5	80	77	92	73	95	82	80	81		52	80
			MY1220	80	83	100	82	0	84	100	81		52	79
			superm2	85	70	94	76	95	80	90	79		51	79
			870715	70	69	98	72	90	83	100	84		51	79
			dyc1997	95	67	62	75	0	77	90	86		47	73
			S2012	70	67	84	77	0	76	64	84		46	71
			6987BBQ	75	68	76	80	0	73	70	80		45	70
			J288118	85	88	84	80	100	0	84	93		43	67
			happy32	0	71	98	71	0	78	0	77		40	62
			jack087	75	69	0	0	100	73	82	76		39	60
			SHA28	80	81	0	0	80	0	60	86		29	45
			60401	65	0	0	0	0	0	0	0		3	5
			hua5840	0	0	0	0	0	0	0	0		0	0

44.2 Line Graph with Markers

Spring 2019 ENG318-01 (Tuesday) Bio03
3/22/2019

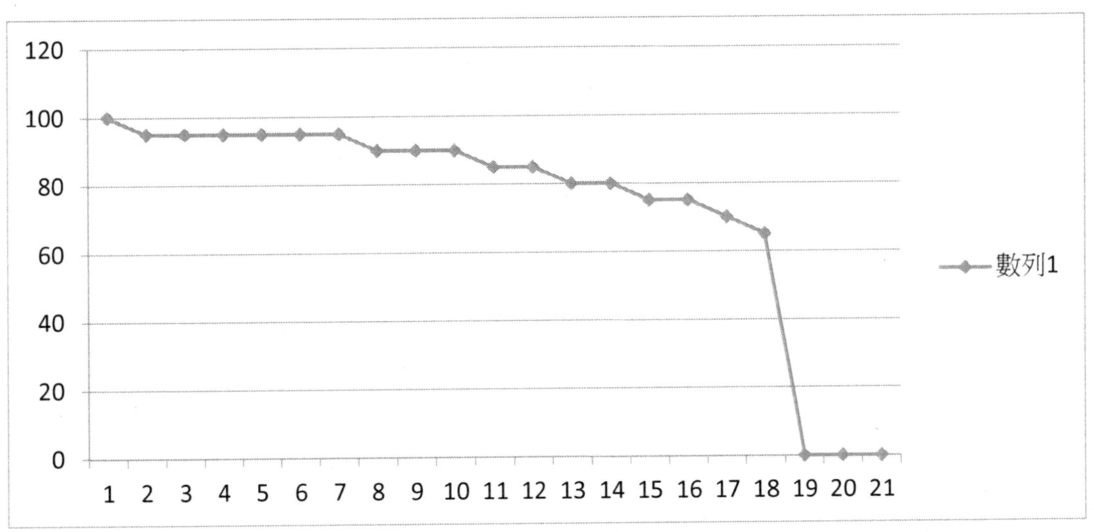

NOTES